A COLDHEARTED KILLER

Flicking the reins, Bob started up the team. As they drove along the edge of the cliff, galloping hoofbeats were heard behind them, coming over the crest of the pass. Patty twisted around to see who was approaching, and recognizing the rider, she smiled and raised a hand in greeting. The smile quickly drained away at the sight of the revolver in his hand. The horseman fired twice, hitting Bob in the back and killing him almost instantly, and Patty screamed in horror as her husband slumped over in the driver's seat. Startled by the gunshots, the team bolted in fear.

The young mother and her children clung to the sides of the wagon as it careened down the steep road behind the galloping team. The road took a sudden turn, and the terrified horses plunged over the cliff. As the wagon sailed into the canyon, Patty's bloodcurdling screams echoed off the mountainside. Finally, after many seconds, there was silence.

The horseman sat his mount, watching impassively. Then reining his horse around, he smiled and headed back to Raton.

The Badge Series
Ask your bookseller for the books you have missed

Book 1: SUNDANCE
Book 2: THE FACELESS MAN
Book 3: THE BLACK COFFIN
Book 4: POWDER RIVER
Book 5: LONDON'S REVENGE
Book 6: THE SHOWDOWN
Book 7: THE IMPOSTOR
Book 8: THE STRANGER
Book 9: BACKLASH
Book 10: BLOOD TRAIL
Book 11: DARK CANYON
Book 12: DEATH LIST
Book 13: THE OUTCAST
Book 14: THE GALLOWS

THE BADGE: BOOK 14

★

THE GALLOWS

★

Bill Reno

Created by the producers of **Wagons West, Stagecoach, Abilene,** and **Faraday.**

Book Creations Inc., Canaan, NY · Lyle Kenyon Engel, Founder

BANTAM BOOKS

NEW YORK • TORONTO • LONDON • SYDNEY • AUCKLAND

THE GALLOWS

*A Bantam Book / published by arrangement with
Book Creations, Inc.*

*Produced by Book Creations, Inc.
Lyle Kenyon Engel, Founder*

Bantam edition / December 1989

ISBN 0-553-28290-5

Published simultaneously in the United States and Canada

Bantam Books are published by Bantam Books, a division of Bantam Doubleday Dell Publishing Group, Inc. Its trademark, consisting of the words "Bantam Books" and the portrayal of a rooster, is Registered in U.S. Patent and Trademark Office and in other countries. Marca Registrada, Bantam Books, 666 Fifth Avenue, New York, New York 10103

PRINTED IN THE UNITED STATES OF AMERICA

O 0 9 8 7 6 5 4 3 2 1

THE GALLOWS

BADGE

While hanging was the usual way to execute a criminal in the Old West, the methods used varied considerably. A town carrying out a judge's sentence usually built a gallows, equipped with a hinged wooden platform, some of which were so elaborate that twelve men could be executed at once. Other less complicated methods involved hanging the sentenced man from a railroad trestle, a bridge, a telegraph pole, or extending a wooden platform from a second-story window. Executions carried out by vigilante committees often centered around a tree from which ropes with nooses were draped.

R. TOELKE '89

Book 14: The Gallows

Chapter One

The citizens of Raton, New Mexico, labored up the steep hill singly and in groups, anger smoldering in their eyes. Looming to the west, the jagged peaks thrust into the clear azure sky, was the Sangre de Cristo range. The rising sun was at their backs, throwing their lengthy shadows before them as they headed toward the crest of the hill . . . and the hanging tree. The tree was a huge cottonwood that stood like a silent sentinel overlooking the mountain town.

The men and women were giving voice to their rage and resentment, while the children, struggling to keep up with their parents, looked on wide-eyed and listened with their mouths agape at how vengeance was about to be exacted on outlaw Leo Dunn. Dunn had led his gang of three men into Raton three days previously to rob the Raton Community Bank, and during the robbery, he had viciously gunned down and killed the bank's president, George Todd.

Town Marshal Dan Washburn had gathered a posse and was in pursuit of the gang almost immediately after they galloped out of town. Within hours Washburn and his men had run the outlaws down, and during the gunfight that ensued, Dunn's three cohorts had been killed. The leader had surrendered when he saw that to carry on the fight was hopeless. As luck would have it, the circuit judge was in town, and Dunn's trial was held the next day. Found guilty of murder, Leo Dunn had been sentenced to hang the following morning, September 4, 1887, from the hanging tree just beyond the west end of town.

Located on the old Sante Fe Trail, Raton had for years been merely an unnamed watering stop for cattlemen and travelers. The town was laid out in 1880, and George Todd came there in early 1881 and established the bank. He had made risky loans to enterprising businessmen who were seeking a start in the new town, and Todd's faith in them and his willingness to take a chance on them had greatly endeared him to the people of Raton. As the majority of Raton's nine hundred residents gathered around the hanging tree that morning, they were pleased that Leo Dunn was going to pay dearly for taking the life of Raton's leading citizen.

Deputy Marshal Ned Mills—who had celebrated his twenty-fifth birthday four months earlier by being hired for his post—came trotting up on his horse, holding the rope that would be used to end Leo Dunn's wicked life. The crowd pressed close around the huge tree as Mills dismounted and flung the hangman's noose over the thick limb that was always used for hangings.

While Mills was anchoring the loose end of the rope to the cottonwood's massive trunk, a boy about ten years of age was heard to whimper to his father, "Pa, I don't like hangings. I don't want to watch. Can I please go home?"

"No, you can't," replied the father. "I want you to grow up to be a good, honest, responsible citizen. Somewhere along the line you may be tempted to take the wrong fork in the road, and if that temptation comes, you'll remember what happens to men who get on the wrong side of the law. Believe me, son, nothing will ever impress you as much as taking in every hanging that happens in this town."

Everyone turned at the approach of a rattling wagon. Driven to the hanging by her neighbors, Alice Todd,

George's middle-aged widow, was wearing a bright red dress to show that to her, Leo Dunn's death was a festive occasion. The wagon drew to a dusty halt, and one man stepped beside the vehicle and helped Alice down.

"You'll feel better in a little while, Alice," promised another man who stood close.

Drawing a handkerchief from her sleeve, Alice dabbed at the tears filling her eyes. "I don't know if I'd call it better, Art, but I will feel relieved," she murmured. "I know that Dunn's neck meeting the end of the rope won't bring my George back, but it is sure going to satisfy the need I have for revenge."

"We'll *all* feel relieved when we see that stinking killer dangling at the end of the rope," put in a small, skinny old man. "We loved George, Alice, and our town will never be the same without him."

Ned Mills, who was just beginning to get to know the people of his newly adopted town, overheard the remarks. One thing he was learning fast: They were a clannish bunch, and they looked out for each other. The deputy removed his hat to wipe his sweating forehead, and the morning breeze ruffled his dark hair. He shot a glance eastward toward town, expecting to see Marshal Dan Washburn escorting the condemned man to the hill, but there was no sign of the funeral wagon as yet—just a few stragglers making their way up the sharp incline.

Mills let his gaze drift over the crowd, not really noticing anyone until he saw beautiful Lisa Washburn. Marshal Washburn's daughter stood beside her mother and her two older brothers and their wives. The same age as Mills, Lisa was sought after by many men but had yet to give her heart to anybody. Ned Mills hoped he would be the one. Knowing how much she adored her father, the deputy hoped that his being a lawman would give him a leg up to win her hand.

Strands of Lisa's honey-blond hair blew across her captivating face, and Mills wanted to dash to her side and brush them away for her. Finally giving in to his impulse to speak to her, the young deputy left the rope to swing in the breeze and headed toward the beautiful blonde and her family. He was within a few yards when someone shouted, "Here they come!"

Mills halted and looked toward the bottom of the hill and saw Wilbur Nicely's funeral wagon begin slowly wending its way up. Since the town's undertaker had to be on hand to take the body away for burial, it had been the custom for the condemned man to ride to the hanging in the same vehicle that would carry away his corpse. Although the wagon was some distance away, and even had he not known in advance who the occupants of the wagon would be, Mills could tell by their builds and coloring who they were. Sitting beside Nicely, his silvering hair gleaming in the sunlight, was Dr. John Townsend, Raton's middle-aged physician, who would pronounce the hanged man dead. Riding in the bed of the wagon were a rawboned Leo Dunn, whose sandy hair—even from that distance—looked lank and greasy, Marshal Dan Washburn, and the marshal's older brother, Abe Washburn, the town's blacksmith and carpenter.

Both Washburn brothers were dark haired, although the lawman was clean-shaven and his brother wore a thick walrus mustache. And while the forty-eight-year-old marshal was of medium height and build, his brother—older by three years—was a giant. As strong as an ox and a bit short-tempered, the older Washburn stood six-feet-four and tipped the scales at just over two hundred and fifty pounds. Because of his size and strength, it had fallen upon Abe Washburn to hoist the condemned man aboard the horse he would ride to his death at the end of the rope.

Every eye in the crowd was fastened on the funeral wagon as it rolled to a halt a few feet from the swaying rope. After setting the brake, the undertaker stepped to the ground, as did Dr. Townsend. Dunn's horse had been secured behind the wagon, and Abe Washburn untied him, then handed the reins to Deputy Mills, who led the animal directly beneath the hangman's rope.

The muscular blacksmith dropped the tailgate and motioned to Leo Dunn with both hands. "Okay," he grunted, "let's go."

Dunn's own hands were shackled behind his back, and he awkwardly dragged himself along the wagon bed. Nearing the tailgate, he suddenly stopped and his body tensed. Marshal Dan Washburn prodded him sharply with an elbow, and Dunn scowled at him, then scooted to the edge of the bed and eased himself to the ground. The lawman then leapt down from the wagon, and flanking the outlaw, the Washburn brothers walked Dunn toward the hanging tree. As they passed, the crowd tightened in a half-circle, pressing as close as they could.

Keeping his eyes on the ground as he walked to his horse, Leo Dunn had not yet looked at the dangling hangman's noose. It was only when he reached his mount that he lifted his face and focused on the ominous noose, and he first stiffened, then his knees buckled slightly. The killer's face took on a ghastly hue, and his tongue nervously licked his dry lips.

Abe Washburn grabbed Dunn by the waist and roughly lifted him up into the saddle. Grinning at the killer, he taunted, "Must be a strange feeling to know you're taking your last ride, huh?"

Dunn did not reply. He only licked his lips again.

Reaching up, Marshal Dan Washburn took hold of the swaying rope and looped the open noose over Leo Dunn's head. The crowd cheered as Washburn cinched it snug around the killer's neck.

Speaking loudly to be heard above the noisy crowd, Dunn told Washburn in a cold, steady voice, "The only difference between you and me, lawman, is you murder with a badge and I murder without one."

Washburn's eyes flashed as he snarled, "There's a big

difference between execution and murder, Dunn." Then, turning away from the outlaw, Dan Washburn asked his deputy, "You got the strap?"

"It's in my left saddlebag," replied Mills.

"I'll get it, Dan," spoke up Abe, moving toward the deputy's horse. The blacksmith reached into the saddlebag and produced a coiled leather strap, then walked back and handed it to his brother.

Dan Washburn let the wide strap unfurl and dangle at his side. Stepping close to the condemned man, he looked up at him and announced so that all in attendance could hear, "Leo Dunn, you have been duly tried and convicted in a court of law for the murder of George Todd. It is therefore my duty to—"

"Murderer! Murderer!" screamed Alice Todd, her emotions exploding. She raced toward Dunn, evading the many hands that tried to restrain her. Reaching the killer, she shrieked, "You filthy beast! You took my George from me! I hope you rot—"

Alice Todd had to jump out of the way to avoid Dunn's horse, which began whinnying and dancing about nervously, causing the rope to pull tight on the killer's neck. While Ned Mills struggled to hold the animal in position, two men seized the distraught widow and pulled her back into the crowd.

Repeating himself, Dan Washburn said loudly, "Leo Dunn, you have been duly tried and convicted in a court of law for the murder of George Todd. It is therefore my duty to hang you as directed by the court. Do you have any last words?"

Leo Dunn choked against the pressure of the noose. Glaring at the marshal, he wheezed, "Yeah. Let's get this over with."

The crowd went still as Marshal Dan Washburn moved to the horse's haunches. The animal's eyes were wild and its ears were laid back, and as Ned Mills gripped the bridle, the gelding's hind legs kept dancing from side to side.

Sweat beaded Leo Dunn's face and he gagged repeatedly, his face turning dark as the noose constricted his windpipe. Swinging the strap to bring it down hard on the horse's rump, Dan shouted to Mills, "Let go, Ned!"

Mills released the bridle, but before the marshal could bring down the strap, the terrified animal reared, pawing the air, then galloped away. Leo Dunn slid from the saddle, swinging freely by his neck, as the rope slowly strangled him. The crowd looked on in horror as the killer dangled a few feet above the ground, his eyes bulging. As he writhed, kicked, and choked, a woman screamed, "Somebody do something!"

The marshal and his deputy looked at each other helplessly, then back at Dunn's contorted and purpled face. Blood began spurting from the outlaw's nostrils, and his mouth spewed saliva.

Alice Todd went into hysterics, screeching incoherently, until someone mercifully carried her away from the scene. Throughout the crowd children were crying and women were fainting, and not a few of the men swayed unsteadily on their feet.

Dr. John Townsend shouted at the lawman, "Marshal, Dunn's agony can go on for several more minutes before he dies! You can't let him suffer like that!"

Abe Washburn stepped beside his brother and offered, "I'll cut the rope where it's tied to the tree if somebody's got a knife."

Shaking his head and drawing his gun, Dan responded, "That'd take too long—and we'd just have to do this all over again. Heaven knows none of us could bear for that to happen!"

The lawman snapped back the hammer of his revolver and tried to aim between the suffering man's eyes, but Dunn was kicking so hard that Washburn could not get a clear shot. Abe immediately wrapped his powerful arms around Dunn's legs and held him still. Men gasped and women screamed as the marshal took dead-center aim and squeezed the trigger. The gun bucked against his palm, and the slug ripped through Leo Dunn's head, spraying the crowd with blood and brain matter.

More women fainted, and several people scattered to give up their breakfasts.

Holstering his gun, Dan Washburn removed his hat, then wiped the sweat from his brow. Breathing deeply, he turned to the undertaker and mumbled, "Wilbur, let's get him down and into the wagon as quickly as possible."

As Wilbur Nicely and a few of the other townsmen got Leo Dunn's body down from the hanging tree, the physician, wiping his own brow, turned to the marshal and groaned, "Dan, that was horrendous."

Washburn shook his head slowly, his face ashen. "I know," he finally responded. Then he turned and faced the crowd, and raising his voice so everyone could hear, he told them, "You've seen hangings here before. You know that normally the condemned man's neck would have been instantly broken when the horse bolted from the sting of the leather. Had that been the case this time, Dunn would have died quickly. We had a very nervous horse here, and things went awry."

"You can say that again," someone in the crowd muttered.

"Maybe it's time to consider building a proper gallows," the physician spoke up, his voice stern.

Looking over at the grotesque body lying in the funeral wagon, the lawman sighed, "I'd say you were right. But for now, the only thing I want to do is get everything back to normal."

He looked at the crowd. "Everybody go on home. The sooner we get back to our usual business, the sooner we'll put the horror we've just witnessed behind us."

The people of Raton seemed almost in a trance as

they slowly descended the steep hill and returned to their homes and businesses. They had never seen a man die in such a horrible manner . . . and none of them would ever forget it.

Chapter Two

Returning to their office after accompanying Leo Dunn's corpse to the funeral parlor, Marshal Dan Washburn and Deputy Ned Mills found Darlene and Lisa Washburn waiting for them. Mother and daughter were seated on a bench on the boardwalk in front of the office, and they rose as the lawmen drew up, walking side by side with Mills leading his horse.

Darlene Washburn—at forty-six, two years younger than her husband—carried her years well, and her blond hair showed only a few streaks of gray. Her daughter was almost a duplicate of her, for they were the same height and proportions, and their facial features were very similar. Everyone who knew the two women were sure that, just like her mother, Lisa would retain her beauty as she grew older.

Quickly stepping beside her husband, Darlene looked at him compassionately and laid a hand on his arm. "Oh, Dan," she murmured, "that must have been awful for you—to have to shoot that man in the head." She shuddered at the grisly memory.

Dan Washburn let out a long, slow breath. "It sure was," he acknowledged. "Hanging a man is unpleasant enough. I hope I never again have to go through another ordeal like that one. Criminals have to be dealt with to the letter of the law, but we certainly need to make sure when we execute a man that he dies quickly."

Lisa kissed her father's cheek, lending her moral support, then gave the deputy a quick but amiable smile.

Mills quickly removed his hat and looked at his boss's daughter, his expression solicitous. "Are you feeling all right after watching that terrible scene?" he asked.

Nodding, Lisa replied softly, "Well enough—although it will be engraved in my mind for a long, long time." Gazing then at her father, she told him solemnly, "Dad, there was a great deal of talk among the people as we were coming down the hill. Everyone was utterly horrified at the way things went."

Lisa Washburn was the apple of her father's eye. Giving her a tender look, he promised, "I'm going to do something about it. Don't you worry." He then patted his daughter on the shoulder and declared, "Well, if you ladies will excuse us, we've got to get to work."

Bidding farewell to the lawmen, the two women headed for home. As soon as they were gone, the marshal and his deputy entered the office. Dan Washburn dropped his hat on the desk and sank wearily into his chair.

Mills hung up his hat on a wall peg and took a chair in front of Dan's desk. "Marshal," he sighed, "I really think we ought to erect a gallows as soon as possible."

"I agree. What I'll do is—"

The marshal's words were interrupted as the door came open and a small Mexican man in his early fifties stepped in. *"Buenos días,"* Manuel Lucero said. He closed the door behind him, then, switching to heavily accented English, asked, "May I see you for a moment, Marshal Washburn?"

"You sure can, Manuel," replied Washburn. "How can I help you?"

Removing his battered felt hat, Manuel ran a hand through his thick gray hair to smooth it. Then he walked across the room and stood in front of the desk, briefly studying the marshal's face. "I was not at the hanging a while ago, Marshal, but some of the people told me about it on the street. I understand it was very bad, eh?"

"It sure was." Dan Washburn peered intently at his visitor and queried, "But that's not why you've come to see me, is it?"

"No," admitted Manuel, grinning. "I wanted to talk to you about Tony before he comes home next week. As I told you when I saw you on the street the other day, he will be paroled next week." Manuel sighed happily. "Finally, after five years, my son will be home."

"I am happy for you, Manuel," Dan offered. "Having your son spend five years in the territorial prison all the way over in Santa Fe cannot have been easy for you."

Smiling, Manuel agreed wryly, "It certainly was not —but now he is being released for good behavior with only one half of his ten-year sentence served. I am going up to Santa Fe next week and pick Tony up." Then the Mexican's face became serious, and he told the lawman, "Marshal, what I want to discuss with you is Tony's threat."

"Oh, you mean the one he made to me before he was taken to prison?"

"*Sí.*" Twisting his hat nervously in his work-worn hands, the Mexican cleared his throat and said, "You will remember, Marshal, that we talked soon after Tony was taken away. I told you then that my son was only speaking in the heat of passion when he threatened you."

Ned Mills asked, "Excuse me, Mr. Lucero, but what did your son threaten Marshal Washburn about?"

Before Manuel could respond, Dan interjected, "I arrested Tony, Ned. Naturally when he was sentenced to ten years in prison, he felt anger toward me."

"If you don't mind my asking," put in the deputy, "what did Tony go to prison for?"

Manuel looked down, shame on his face, as Dan replied, "He tried to kill a man named Dominic Ortega.

The two men were drinking in one of the saloons. Tony got extremely drunk, and when Ortega irritated him, Tony went after him. Ortega pulled a knife, but Tony took it away from him and in a rage, stabbed him three times. Ortega lived, but the circuit judge sentenced Tony to ten years for attempted murder."

Manuel Lucero looked at the younger lawman. His eyes were filled with pleading as he murmured, "Deputy Mills, you must understand that my boy had never done anything like that before. He . . . well, he showed a tendency toward violence only when he got drunk. Believe me, he has learned his lesson. I have received many letters from him, and in each letter he told me that he will never again touch another drop of alcohol as long as he lives."

"When did Tony make this threat to the marshal, Mr. Lucero?"

Manuel sighed. "It . . . it was the day he was sentenced to prison. After the trial, Marshal Washburn was escorting him back to the jail—and that was when Tony threatened him." Looking down at the floor again, he continued in a soft voice, "He told the marshal he would get even with him as soon as he was released from prison."

"Was he drunk then?"

Manuel's head came up. "No," he admitted. Shifting nervously on his feet, he assured the deputy, "This was different. My Tony was very angry, you understand. He was facing ten years in prison. The marshal, he was the one who chased him down and captured him."

In a disgusted tone Mills retorted, "Tony had no call to be angry at the marshal, Mr. Lucero! Dan Washburn didn't pour the liquor down his throat, nor did Dan Washburn put the knife in his hand!"

The marshal leaned forward in his chair and said, "Easy, Ned. Don't be so rough on Manuel. He's suffered a lot because of this, and so have his wife and their two daughters. If Tony told his father that he's learned his lesson and is never going to touch liquor again, that's good enough for me. Before the stabbing incident Tony was a model citizen—and the prison officials are letting him out on parole because he's been a model citizen inside those walls as well. Sounds to me like Tony has learned his lesson—and I, for one, am willing to give him a chance to prove that he wants to do right."

Manuel Lucero's expression was cool as he gazed at the deputy. In a flat, steady voice he stated, "I have talked to my son about the threat he made to Marshal Washburn. He assures me he holds no ill will against the marshal, and that his words of revenge were rash and made in the heat of anger." Then, turning to Washburn, his face softening, he explained, "Marshal, this is why I came here just now. I just wanted to assure you that you have nothing to worry about."

"I appreciate your coming, Manuel," Dan replied, smiling. "You tell Tony that I said bygones are bygones. If he wants to come back and live in Raton, he is welcome."

Manuel clapped the old hat on his head and reached across the desk to shake hands with the marshal. "Thank you, Marshal Washburn!" he told the lawman effusively as their hands clasped. "Thank you! I will tell Tony what you said. Everything is going to be all right, now. Mama and I will have our boy back, and everything will be wonderful again!"

Turning, he walked briskly to the door. As he stepped outside Dr. John Townsend came rushing up. The Mexican nodded at the doctor and continued on his way, and Townsend entered.

The physician's face was grim, and as he strode across the room, his eyes fixed on the marshal, he declared, "Dan, I've listened to a lot of people in the last few minutes, and let me tell you, that horrid scene at the hanging has taken its toll on them. Many of them are even saying they want no more executions in Raton."

Dan stiffened. "That's foolish talk, Doc. That would only invite more crime."

"I think so, too," conceded the physician, "but I thought you would want to know what's going on in our fellow citizens' minds."

Washburn relaxed and eased back in his chair. "Frankly, I don't blame the people for not wanting to see another execution like the one they witnessed today. What we need is a gallows to insure that death is always instantaneous." He leaned forward, elbows on the desk. "Tell you what. I'll call for a town meeting and ask everyone to approve the building of one right away. Besides, it's time we had something more permanent. Raton is growing, and we'll soon have a thousand people living here. I know it's not something people like to think about, but let's face it, sometimes progress means things other than new shops or streetlamps."

Nodding, Townsend conceded, "You're right about that." He turned to leave and added, "I'm glad you agree that something needs to be done, Dan."

"I do, indeed." Standing, the lawman put on his Stetson and walked to the door with the physician. "Tell you what. In order not to waste another minute, I'm going to see Weston DeRose right now."

Weston DeRose, who was quite successful in business and well-off financially, was Raton's town council chairman. A short, stout man of fifty-five with a thick head of graying brown hair, DeRose was standing beside his desk with an unlit cigar clamped between his teeth as the marshal walked into his office. Turning from the file drawer he was riffling through when he heard the marshal enter, DeRose smiled at the lawman. He closed the file drawer and said, "Howdy, Dan. What can I do for you?"

Dan Washburn explained the need for a town meeting to call for the erection of a gallows.

DeRose nodded. "I agree, Dan. As long as human

nature remains what it is, there are going to be outlaws and killers. We may just as well be prepared for them."

"How soon can we set up a town meeting?" asked the marshal.

DeRose stroked his chin for a few moments, then remarked, "Well, I've got to leave town for a few days. Have some business to attend to over in Clayton. In fact, I'll be leaving in about half an hour. So you might want to go ahead and have the town meeting without me."

Shaking his head, Dan declared, "No, you're the community leader of Raton, and I'll need you at the meeting in case we have some dissenters." He paused, then asked, "This is Monday. When will you be back?"

"Friday morning," answered DeRose. "We could have the meeting Friday night."

"Good enough," Dan confirmed. "I'll put out the word that we'll be having a town meeting at seven o'clock Friday night, and everyone should attend, if possible."

Leaving DeRose's office, Marshal Dan Washburn had just closed the door behind him when he heard a ruckus going on a block away. He hurried toward the commotion and saw a crowd gathering in front of the Raton General Store.

The marshal pushed his way through the gathering of people in the middle of the street and found his oldest son, Bob, in a shouting match with Dexter Finn, owner of the Lucky Dog Saloon. Bob was coowner with his brother, Dave—younger by one year—of the successful Raton General Store. From behind, the twenty-eight-year-old Bob was often mistaken for both his father and his brother, for all three men had the same build and sported identical mops of dark hair. It was the family joke that Dan and Darlene had made a deal before the children were born that any boys would look just like him, while girls would look like their mother.

Striding up to the two men, whose shouts threatened

to erupt into a fist fight, Dan stepped between them. "All right, you two!" he growled. "Settle down and tell me what this is all about." He looked from one man to the other. Dexter Finn's compact, stocky body stiffened, and he twirled the end of his bushy mustache but said nothing.

Bob Washburn's scowl suddenly turned into a grin. "Actually, we're fighting about you, Dad."

"Me? What in the world for?"

Bob's face became serious again as he gestured with his thumb at Finn and announced, "He was bad-mouthing you, Dad. Said it was your fault Leo Dunn died in such an awful manner."

"Well, it was!" rasped Finn, glaring at the marshal. "You saw that Dunn's horse was acting up before you took the strap in your hand. You should've settled the animal down before proceeding with the execution."

"I've seen horses skittish before, Dexter," parried Dan defensively. "The execution would have gone off just fine if Alice Todd hadn't jumped in screaming."

"Oh, so now you're shoving the blame off on poor Alice, huh?" Sweat glistened on Finn's bald pate as the saloon owner stood there bristling, his hands on his hips.

"I'm not blaming Alice for anything!" the marshal retorted sharply. "She was upset—and rightfully so. But the fact remains that when she jumped at Dunn, the horse went over the edge with fright. There was no way I could control what happened."

"Sure," mocked Finn.

Bob Washburn's face hardened. Moving toward the saloon owner again, he roared, "I'm gonna shut your big mouth for you, Finn!"

Dan blocked Bob with an elbow, saying, "No need for that, son. You and I both know that his problem goes a lot deeper than the incident this morning."

"Everybody in this town knows that," spat Bob, fixing Finn with a withering look. "You don't like it that Dan Washburn holds a tight rein on troublemakers . . . and your saloon seems to draw troublemakers. Dad runs them off, then you criticize him behind his back."

"With good reason!" snapped the saloon owner. "Just because some of my customers get a little rowdy when they come in and drink doesn't mean he ought to storm into my place every time and run 'em off or jail 'em!"

"We have laws in this town about disturbing the peace," the marshal said calmly. "When your customers —or anybody else—break those laws, I handle them as I see fit to preserve the peace."

"Yeah!" snarled Finn. "And word's gotten around! So a lot of men ride to nearby towns to do their drinking instead of coming to the Lucky Dog. Your straitlaced ways are costing me money, and I don't like it."

Keeping his voice low, Dan Washburn looked the saloonkeeper in the eye and commented, "Well, I guess you could go into another business, Dexter—or if you want to stay in the saloon business, you could pack up and find another town. Ted Willis doesn't seem to mind my straitlaced ways. His saloon is doing just fine."

Finn mumbled something under his breath.

"What'd you say?" asked the marshal.

Lancing Washburn with piercing eyes, Finn grunted, "I said maybe what this town needs is a new marshal."

Dan bristled. "I was here before you set foot in Raton, mister, and I'll be here after you're gone," he retorted.

Finn pivoted and began walking away. Over his shoulder he called loudly, "That remains to be seen, Washburn."

No one moved until Dexter Finn had entered his saloon. As soon as he was out of sight, the crowd began to disperse. Several people, however, approached the marshal and assured him they would back him to the hilt. Feeling vindicated, Marshal Dan Washburn returned to his office.

Abe Washburn's blacksmith and carpentry shop was near the south end of town. When the Washburn brothers moved to Raton in 1880, Dan became the town's first marshal, while Abe opened his shop. The hulking man had dark brown hair the same shade as Dan's, but the brotherly resemblance stopped there. Big and strong, Abe's wide-set eyes and thick, broad features made him downright ugly, and his thick mustache gave him a somewhat animallike appearance. Dan had worried that Abe would never find a woman who would love him, but to his surprise, a sweet—though rather plain—woman came into his life. Sadly, after just a few years of marriage, Bertha had died some ten years previously, leaving Abe alone again, for they had had no children.

When the Washburn brothers had first headed west together from Illinois some thirty years before, they initially settled in Pampa, Texas, where Dan became deputy marshal. Abe had entertained big dreams of somehow becoming wealthy in Texas, but nothing seemed to jell. He finally settled down to work with his hands, which came naturally to him, opening a blacksmith and carpentry shop.

The two brothers both met their wives in the small Texas town—although Abe had to wait a number of years longer. Dan was made marshal of Pampa in 1864, serving happily there for many years. Then, late in 1879, word came that a settlement in northern New Mexico Territory was being incorporated into a town and would need a marshal. Dan got excited about moving farther west, as did his family. Making a trip to the settlement, he offered to become their marshal when the town was established, and he was duly hired. By the time Dan and his family were ready to leave Pampa, Abe was a widower, and the elder Washburn decided to go with his brother. He once again established a combination blacksmithy and carpentry shop, and almost from the moment he opened his doors in Raton, Abe Washburn's business did modestly well.

The huge man was hammering out a horseshoe when

Manuel Lucero stepped through the big double doors of the shop. Manuel waited while the blacksmith labored at forming the red-hot shoe. When Abe was finally satisfied with his handiwork and dipped it into a bucket of cool water, the small Mexican approached the huge man. "I was wondering how you are coming with my wagon, Señor Abe," he asked.

As the horseshoe hissed and sent up steam from the bucket, Abe gestured with his chin toward the vehicle on the other side of the shop. "I'll have it ready day after tomorrow, first thing in the morning, Manuel."

The Mexican grinned and replied, "That will be fine, Señor Abe. That will give me enough time to reach Santa Fe by the time Tony gets out Monday afternoon."

Abe lifted the horseshoe out of the water, examined it for a few seconds, then placed the shoe back in the water. Clearing his throat, he muttered, "Manuel, there's something I want to ask you."

"What is that?"

The blacksmith looked intently at the smaller man. "I want to know if my brother's in any danger."

"You are speaking of my son's threat to get even, Señor Abe?"

"That's what I'm talking about," confirmed the big man.

"I have just come from the marshal's office, where I assured your brother that Tony meant nothing by his threat," Manuel informed him.

"A lot of people heard him say it," Abe reminded him. "That includes me. Tony sure sounded like he meant it."

Manuel sighed and repeated what he had told the lawman. Then he declared, "Tony very much wants to come back to Raton and make a life here—and I hope the people will let him do it. He just wants to live a good and productive life."

"I'm glad to hear that," Abe intoned. "I'll tell you this

much: If Tony is really serious about living right, I'll be the first to help him."

"Thank you, Señor Abe," Manuel breathed. "This means very much to me. Well, then, I will be back the day after tomorrow to pick up my wagon. *Adiós.*"

That evening a full moon lit the sky as the entire Washburn clan—with the exception of Abe—sat down to a hearty meal at Dan and Darlene Washburn's house. Aside from the usual occupants of the house—the marshal, his wife, and his daughter—present also were Bob and his pretty brunette wife, Patty, and their two young children; and Dave and his lovely blond wife, Wilma, who was five months pregnant with their first child.

Dan sat at one end of the long table and Darlene at the other. While the meal was being devoured by all but two-year-old Mary Jane—who seemed to be getting more food *on* herself than *in* herself—the guests pointedly refrained from discussing the horrid scene at the hanging tree. Bob raised the argument between Dexter Finn and himself, and looking at the marshal, he asked, "Dad, what do you suppose Finn meant? You know, when you told him you had been here before he came and would be here after he was gone, and he said, 'That remains to be seen'? Do you think he's going to try to cause some kind of trouble for you?"

Dan shook his head, admitting, "I'm not exactly sure —and frankly, he may not be sure, either. I can't believe it means much, though. He was probably just spouting off."

"Speaking of trouble," spoke up Lisa, "I know you told us that Manuel Lucero is certain there won't be any for you from Tony, but what about between Tony and Juan Gomez? Tony sure can't be happy that Dolores Domingo has broken their engagement and plans to marry another man."

The Washburns all nodded in agreement, murmuring among themselves. Before he had been arrested and sent to prison, Tony was engaged to Dolores, who lived in town with her widowed aunt, Flora Domingo. On the day Tony left under guard for Santa Fe, Dolores had told him she would wait for his return, declaring that she loved him so dearly that even ten years apart could not change her love.

Recently, a young Mexican named Juan Gomez had come to Raton, and he began paying a great deal of attention to Dolores. Starved for male companionship after five years—and now realizing how long another five years would be—Dolores allowed him to court her. Juan had proposed marriage only a short time before, and Dolores accepted his proposal. They set the date for the first of November.

Everyone in town knew that Dolores had written to Tony, telling him that she was now engaged to Juan Gomez, but there had been no response from Tony. Dolores had been shocked when, two weeks after she had agreed to marry Juan, it was announced that Tony was going to be released five years sooner than she had expected.

Dan Washburn took a sip of coffee, placed the cup back in its saucer, and responded to Lisa, "I don't know, honey. All I do know is that Manuel assured me Tony wants to live in Raton and be a responsible citizen. Certainly if he attacks Juan Gomez, it would hardly be a responsible act." He sighed. "All we can do is wait and see. I'm hoping Tony will be exactly as Manuel describes him—repentant and eager to begin fresh."

Suddenly there was a knock at the front door. Darlene Washburn looked toward the door, then at her daughter. "That's probably Ned, Lisa."

As Lisa pushed her chair back and stood up, Dave grinned and quipped, "Your faithful suitor, eh?"

"No. Dad's faithful deputy," the blonde retorted drily, dropping her napkin on the table.

As Lisa walked past him, Dan reached out and took

her arm. "Honey," he said softly, "if you don't want Ned around, I'll tell him not to bother you."

The knock was repeated, this time louder.

"It isn't that I don't like Ned, Dad," replied the lovely blonde, "but even though I've only known him a short time, he's already proposed marriage. I don't wish to be rude to him, but while I'm fond of him, I'm definitely not in love with him, and I never will be. To be honest, I think he lacks character and manhood. I'm not sure whether he can be a good lawman, much less a good husband."

Dan shook his head. "Well, I must admit I'd prefer it if he had a bit more gumption and—"

The knock came again. Dan released Lisa's arm and let her head for the door. Moments later Lisa returned with the deputy at her heels. Mills greeted everyone with a warm smile, then asked Lisa if they could take a walk together in the moonlight. Lisa reluctantly accepted and threw on a light shawl, and after telling her parents she would not be long, she headed out the door with the deputy right behind her.

As Lisa Washburn and Ned Mills strolled the streets of Raton, she was glad to be out in the cool night air. She was still upset from witnessing Leo Dunn's awful death, and the air helped to refresh her.

They walked north a few blocks, then started home, and soon they were back at the Washburn front porch. Lisa was about to bid Ned good-night when he looked longingly into her eyes and took hold of her hand. She stiffened a bit and pulled her hand free.

"Please, Ned," she told him, her voice kind. "I must be getting in. I've got to get to bed."

"So early?" he asked.

"Yes. I've promised Bob and Dave that I'll help them take inventory at the store in the morning. It'll only take about three hours, but I have to be there at six o'clock. So I really must go in now."

The deputy's face fell. "Lisa," he breathed, "you must

give me an answer soon. I'm so in love with you, and I want you for my wife. Please say you'll marry me."

Lisa sighed. "Ned, you mustn't press me like this. I like you, and I enjoy being with you, but I am just not ready to discuss marriage."

Looking pained, Mills asked, "Is there someone else, Lisa?"

"No, there isn't anyone else. I'm simply not ready to become engaged . . . to you or anyone."

The lovely blonde hoped that some other young woman would come along and steal Ned's heart. She had wanted many times to explain that her feelings toward him were merely sisterly and always would be, but she refrained, knowing how much it would hurt him. So she decided to try to ride out their relationship until Ned got discouraged and dropped her—or fell in love with someone else.

Giving him a peck on the cheek, she bade him good-night and opened the door. As she was closing it she watched Ned Mills head toward his house, whistling a happy tune. It was clear that he was still hopeful that Lisa would one day be his.

Chapter Three

Shortly before nine o'clock the next morning, Lisa Washburn stood in the doorway of the Raton General Store, chatting with her brother Bob. The inventory was finished, and their brother, Dave, was in the storeroom at the back, breaking open some new boxes.

Bob leaned down, kissed his sister on the forehead and said, "Thanks, Sis. You've been a great help. Inventory always goes so much smoother and faster when you're here."

Smiling, the blonde replied, "You are so welcome, my darling brother. Anytime you and Dave need some assistance, just let me know."

Turning back into the store, Bob told his sister, "See you later."

Lisa stepped out onto the boardwalk and started toward home. There was a good deal of traffic on Main Street, with wagons, buggies, riders on horseback, and many pedestrians milling about the business district. A young female voice called Lisa's name from across the street. Looking in that direction, the blonde raised a hand and waved at her friend. She started to cross over when the rumble of galloping hooves sounded from the north. Turning her head, she saw people and animals scattering, making way for three riders who were thundering into town from the direction of Raton Pass.

Lisa stood at the edge of the boardwalk, waiting until

the riders passed by to cross. But the man in the lead shouted something over his shoulder to the two men following him and suddenly reined his heavily lathered, foam-flecked mount in her direction. Without warning, the leader jumped his gasping horse onto the wooden planking and leaned from his saddle, snatching Lisa onto the horse with him. The young woman screamed and fought him, demanding he put her down, but the man's strength was too great. Clutching her against him, he spurred his horse off the boardwalk back into the street and bolted southward, his two companions racing immediately behind him.

Raton's main street instantly erupted into bedlam. Some people shouted Lisa's name while they watched the three horses disappear from view, while others argued with each other about what to do. Several men said they should get on their horses immediately and pursue Lisa and her captors, but some of the others cautioned they must advise Dan Washburn of his daughter's abduction and let him decide on a course of action. Two men then dashed toward the marshal's office, leaving the rest of the shocked citizens to their confusion.

Bob and Dave Washburn emerged from the general store to see what all the excitement was about, and they were stunned to learn that their sister had been kidnapped. Bob turned to his brother and exclaimed, "Let's get Dad and go after them!"

Before Dave could reply, the two men who had run to the marshal's office returned, out of breath, saying that neither the marshal nor his deputy were to be found.

Abe Washburn suddenly appeared, a hammer dangling from one hand. "What's going on?" he asked.

A babel of voices answered him, further informing him that neither lawman was around.

"They're out at Gifford Hornsby's place a few miles east of here," Abe rejoined. "I was in Dan's office when one of Hornsby's kids came in to get them, saying his pa was beating up his mother and brother. Dan thought he might need Ned's help to restrain Hornsby."

"Then we've got to act on our own," advised Dave Washburn, looking around at the crowd. "Most of you men already have your guns on. Bob and I will get ours, then saddle our horses and meet you here in a few minutes. We'll—"

"You people!" a voice shouted, and everyone turned to see a lone rider barreling down the street from the north. He skidded his lathered, snorting mount to a halt, and the rawboned man's U.S. marshal's badge glinted on his vest. The federal man, who looked to be in his early thirties, sat tall in his saddle as he ran his pale blue eyes over the gathering of citizens. Whipping off his Stetson, he wiped his sweating forehead and sandy-colored hair and mustache with his sleeve. "Any of you folks see three riders come through town a few minutes ago?" he asked breathlessly, placing the hat back on.

"They were just here, Marshal," replied Bob Washburn excitedly. "They grabbed my sister and took off with her!" Pointing, he added, "They headed straight south out of town. We were just making plans to saddle up and go after them."

The federal man tugged thoughtfully on his neatly trimmed mustache. "Doesn't Raton have a marshal?" he queried.

"Yes, sir," the shopkeeper responded. "As a matter of fact, he's my father—Dan Washburn. I'm his eldest son, Bob, and this is my brother, Dave. Dad's out of town right now, and his deputy is with him. I assume you're chasing those three men."

"Sure am. My name is Ben Bryce, and I work out of the U.S. marshal's office down in El Paso. I've been chasing those three cold-blooded killers for two weeks. Followed them into Colorado, and then they doubled back on me and headed over Raton Pass. You say they kidnapped your sister? Well, there's no time to waste.

Those men are desperate—which means your sister is in real danger."

"We'll get our horses and guns and ride with you, Marshal," spoke up Dave.

"No, I can make better time alone," Bryce responded. "Their horses are as tired as mine, so if I could borrow a fresh mount, I can catch up with them."

"You can have mine, Marshal," volunteered a young man in the crowd. "I just trotted him into town from my place a half mile out, so he's all warmed up and ready to go. He's plenty fast, too."

"Good!" exclaimed the federal man, swinging from his saddle and pulling his Winchester .44 repeater from its boot. Following the young man to his waiting steed, the tall, muscular lawman leapt into the saddle. He glanced over at Bob Washburn and told him, "Get word to your father as soon as possible. Tell him to follow me." The lawman then reined the horse around, about to head off, when he paused and asked, "Your sister, is she a child?"

"No, Marshal," replied Bob. "She's twenty-five."

Bryce nodded, spurred the bay gelding, and rode hard in pursuit of the gang.

The three outlaws pushed their exhausted horses mercilessly along the dusty road. Guy Durfee held Lisa Washburn in front of him, gripping her tightly around her waist. Twisting her body furiously in an attempt to free herself from her captor's grip, Lisa begged, "Let me go! Please let me go!"

"Not a chance, girlie," Durfee growled. "You're far too useful."

Lisa's pretty face grew angry. "My father is marshal of Raton!" she shouted. "When he learns what's happened, he'll come after you—and you'll regret this!"

Durfee threw back his head and laughed. "You'd better hope for his sake that he don't catch us—'cause if he does, *he's* the one who'll be sorry."

The three men were riding abreast, and Dorsey Casteel suddenly pointed out, "These animals ain't gonna last much longer. We've got to find some fresh horses."

"There must be a ranch somewhere along this road," put in Roger Vining. "First one we come to, we'll pull in and grab us some horses."

A quarter mile farther, a small ranch came into view. The house, barn, and a cluster of outbuildings were situated some sixty yards from the road, and several horses were in the corral next to the barn.

"Hey, boys!" shouted Durfee, pointing toward the place. "Look over there! We'll get us four of them horses—one for the marshal's pretty daughter!"

"You don't need me!" Lisa cried. "Please, I beg of you, let me go. Besides, I'll just slow you down."

"Slow us down, nothin'!" blurted Durfee. "Honey, you better get used to bein' a prisoner, 'cause you're our ticket to freedom. We got us a stinkin' federal marshal on our tails, and whenever he gets too close, you'll be the perfect shield to hold him at bay. He ain't gonna start shootin' when he sees you and take the chance of blowin' your pretty head off."

The three outlaws turned their exhausted horses off the road and headed toward the cluster of buildings. Bypassing the house, they made for the barn and hauled up beside the corral gate. As he slid from his saddle, Casteel began loosening the cinch under his horse's belly and ordered, "Guy, you hold the woman. Roger and I will get these saddles off, then we'll take us four fresh steeds. There's bound to be gear in the barn for the woman's horse."

While Casteel and Vining were removing the saddles and bridles from the weary horses, Durfee kept a firm grip on Lisa. Noticing her looking toward the ranch house, he sneered, "You ain't goin' nowhere, missy, so just stand still."

Suddenly the back door of the house swung open, and the rancher, Larry Stack, came storming off the porch bearing a double-barreled shotgun. His face was beet-red as he roared, "Hey! Just what the heck do you men think you're doing?"

Stepping in front of Lisa, Durfee sneered and announced, "We're borrowin' your horses, that's what."

"Get away from my corral!" Stack bellowed. "I'm warning you, if you think you're going to take any of those horses, you'd better guess again! Get back on your animals and ride! Right now! Get off my prop—"

The young rancher noticed Lisa Washburn. Looking shocked, he automatically lowered his weapon, demanding, "Lisa, what on earth is going on?"

Suddenly two guns spit fire. Hit in the chest, Larry Stack went down, dropping his shotgun. Lisa shrieked as the rancher twitched a few times, then lay still. Gasping, she wrenched out of Durfee's grasp and glared at Casteel and Vining, who stood holding smoking guns. "You didn't have to kill him!" she screamed at the top of her voice. "How could you do such a cold-blooded thing? You—"

Guy Durfee's flat palm stung Lisa's mouth as he bellowed, "Shut your trap, woman!"

Casteel and Vining were about to turn toward the corral when the rancher's wife raced out of the house, carrying a small child in her arms. Screaming wildly, she ran toward her husband lying on the ground, but the outlaws fired at her, the bullets chewing wood as they bit into the house. Donna Stack screamed again and dashed back inside, and through the open window she could be heard crying out her husband's name.

Grabbing Lisa, Durfee dragged her toward the corral, and as he did so, he saw U.S. Marshal Ben Bryce coming on fast. Durfee swore and shouted to his cohorts, "It's Bryce! He's caught up with us!"

Casteel and Vining whirled and spotted the lawman. Casteel hollered, "Into the barn, Guy! Hurry! Bring the woman!"

Lisa struggled against Guy Durfee's strong hands as

he dragged her into the barn. Dorsey Casteel pulled the door shut behind them and slid the bolt in place, plunging the interior of the barn into virtual darkness. The barn was redolent with the strong scent of old wood, leather harness, and stale manure, and the only light was that which seeped through knotholes and cracks and from a tiny window above the hayloft.

Roger Vining groped his way toward the wall that faced the house, stumbling twice against unseen objects. Peering through a knothole, he called over his shoulder, "I'll keep Bryce in sight, fellas. You two position yourselves so you can cover the door."

"Right," answered Casteel.

Their eyes adjusting to the dark, the two outlaws began pushing feed barrels together to further barricade the door. Guy Durfee held on to Lisa Washburn with one hand, but as he made his way to the far wall, he stumbled and his grip on her arm eased. As swift as a cat, Lisa wrenched her arm loose and darted for the big door. Swearing, Durfee ran after her, shouting, "Don't let her get away!"

Lisa had gone only a few steps when her feet tangled in something on the floor and she went down head over heels. Breathing heavily, she scrambled to her feet, straining toward the rectangular thread of light that outlined the door. She had gotten only another two steps farther when strong hands seized her and whirled her around.

"You try that again, lady," warned Durfee, "and I'll kill you with my bare hands!"

Outside, Ben Bryce drew his horse to a halt alongside the dead rancher and pulled his rifle from the boot. As he slid from his saddle he heard a woman wailing and paused. Should he head for the barn, where he had seen the outlaws drag the blond woman, or toward the house? He saw the door of the house start to open, and he raced toward the porch just as Donna Stack stepped outside. "You better stay in the house," the marshal cautioned the distraught young woman.

"Is . . . is my husband dead?" she asked in a small voice, her face twisted with grief.

Bryce gently guided her back inside. "I'm afraid so, ma'am. Please. Stay inside, for the sake of your baby."

Bryce then bounded off the porch and ran toward the barn. Noting that the outlaws had stripped their mounts of their tack, which lay on the ground, as a precaution he loosened the cinch on his own horse just enough so if a man stepped into the stirrup, the saddle would swing down and dump him on the ground.

Carrying the Winchester, he levered a cartridge into the chamber and cautiously eased across the yard. Suddenly the muzzle of a revolver popped through a knothole, and then the gun boomed and a slug whined past Bryce's head. Raising his rifle quickly, he took aim and sent a .44 slug about three inches to the right of the smoking knothole. He heard a cry of pain. Working the lever rapidly, he sent another shot about six inches below the first one. There was a strangled cry, then silence.

Suddenly Dorsey Casteel's voice thundered from the interior of the barn. "Bryce, you better back off! We've got a woman with us, and if you don't ride outta here this minute, we'll kill her!"

Ben Bryce stared hard at the barn. He knew the men he was dealing with. He did not know which one he had hit, nor if he was dead, but there were definitely two others holding Marshal Dan Washburn's daughter as hostage—and they were heartless killers without conscience. When they were through using her, they would kill her, which meant that the situation left no alternative. He had to go in there and rescue the young woman immediately.

Inside the barn the two outlaws hunkered behind the feed barrels with Lisa Washburn between them. Casteel said in a low voice, "Guy, I think Roger's dead. If he was alive, we'd hear him breathin'."

"Yeah," agreed Durfee.

"You stay here and keep a good hold on this female," said Casteel. "I'm gonna check on the marshal."

Dorsey Casteel made his way through the shadowed interior of the barn toward the spot where Roger Vining had stood. Reaching his cohort, he leaned down and felt for a pulse on the side of Vining's neck. There was none. Calling softly to Durfee that Roger was dead, he stood up and peered through a knothole. Ben Bryce was nowhere in sight.

"See anything?" Durfee asked.

"Nope. I wonder if we scared him off."

"I seriously doubt that," came Durfee's dry reply.

"Yeah. Me, too. But I can't see him or his horse. He could be hidin' behind that shed out there. His horse could be there, too. I—"

With a sudden crash the federal man plunged through a small door in the side of the barn and hit the floor rolling. The door rebounded off the wall and slammed shut, leaving the barn as dark as before. Bryce's act had taken both outlaws off guard and without time to send a shot in his direction. Now neither of them dared make a sound and make his position known.

Realizing that Lisa Washburn could give away his location, Guy Durfee clamped his hand over the young woman's mouth. But the spunky blonde twisted her head, managing to get one of his fingers between her teeth, and bit down with all her might. Durfee howled with pain.

The outlaw jerked his finger free, but before he could muffle her again, Lisa cried out, "Over here, Marshal!"

Creeping slowly toward her voice, his eyes not yet adjusted to the darkness, Ben Bryce bumped into a pitchfork, which clattered to the floor, and Guy Durfee sent a shot in that direction. The sharp sound reverberated through the barn, and the place quickly filled with the acrid smell of burnt gunpowder. Bryce saw Durfee's form lighted briefly by the orange flash and caught a glimpse of the woman's head next to him. He held his fire, hoping for a clear view of the outlaw, and as he crawled closer to Durfee in the deep shadows, he wondered where the other outlaw was.

The federal man inched his way along the wall, guided by Lisa's muffled yet heavy breathing. In his hand was his Colt .45, cocked and ready to fire, which gave him more maneuverability than the rifle he had left outside.

Suddenly Bryce's leg brushed against a pile of straw, and the lawman cursed inwardly. The outlaw had clearly heard the crackling sound, for a split second later, a shot came from Durfee's direction. The bullet ripped through Bryce's left side, but he ignored the burning pain long enough to level his muzzle and return fire at Guy Durfee, who had been clearly illuminated by the flash from his gun. Bryce's bullet tore into Durfee's head, killing him instantly. From where he stood, the marshal heard Lisa Washburn whimper with relief when the outlaw fell.

From the other side of the barn came the sound of a bolt being slid back, and then the barn was suddenly flooded with light as Dorsey Casteel dashed outside. Ben Bryce's revolver boomed, and the slug tore splinters from the doorframe. Giving Lisa a quick, reassuring look, Bryce then staggered out the door after the outlaw.

Rounding the corner, gun ready, the marshal took aim at Casteel as the man leapt onto Bryce's borrowed horse. But the loosened cinch immediately slid under the outlaw's weight, leaving the animal dancing about with the loose saddle dangling under its belly and Dorsey Casteel dumped on the ground. Still gripping his gun, the outlaw rolled onto his side and brought his weapon to bear on Bryce.

The federal man already had a bead on Casteel, and

he warned, "Don't try it, mister!" But the marshal saw by the look in Dorsey Casteel's eyes that he was going to shoot, and he dropped his hammer.

The impact of the slug knocked the outlaw backward as a huge crimson splotch slowly spread over his chest. His legs twitched a couple of times, then he lay still.

Ben Bryce suddenly sagged to his knees, clutching his bleeding side. He felt the gun slip from his fingers as the whole world spun around him. Then gentle hands were on his shoulders, easing him onto the ground. Looking up, he saw Lisa Washburn kneeling beside him, and he told her weakly, "I guess I must have died and gone to heaven, 'cause anyone as gorgeous as you has to be an angel."

Lisa gave the federal man a brief, small smile, then told him, "Hush. Lie still so I can look at your wound."

Working gently, Lisa ripped his shirt open. "The bullet passed on through, Marshal, but I'd guess that it really tore you up because you're bleeding heavily. I'll bind it as best I can, and then I'll get you into town to the doctor." She began ripping lengths of her petticoat to use as bandage.

The door of the house opened, and the rancher's wife stepped onto the porch. She paused, staring at her husband's corpse, then slowly made her way across the yard. With the baby held tight to her breast, Donna Stack knelt beside her dead husband and sobbed.

The young blonde looked over at the newly widowed woman, and her eyes filled with tears. She then refocused on her task. The federal man watched her with steady eyes, telling her, "When I stopped in town, they told me you're the marshal's daughter."

"That's right," she replied. "I'm surprised my father didn't come after me with you."

"Your brothers told me he and his deputy were out at a ranch a few miles from town. I told them to get word to him as soon as possible. I'm sure he'll be along soon."

Lisa did not respond. She was intently concentrating on stemming the flow of blood from Bryce's wound.

"Your brothers didn't tell me your name, ma'am," Bryce remarked.

"Lisa," answered the blonde, keeping her eyes on her work.

"Lisa," he echoed. "Right pretty name—for a right beautiful lady."

Lisa blushed but said nothing. A few moments later she instructed, "Press the cloth against the wound as tight as you can. You'll have to hold it there until we get you to Dr. Townsend." She stood up and glanced across the yard. "I've got to see to Donna."

Lisa hurried to Donna Stack and knelt down beside her, trying her best to comfort her.

A few minutes had passed when the sound of galloping hooves came from the direction of the road. Seconds later, Marshal Dan Washburn and Deputy Ned Mills thundered into the yard. As the lawmen skidded their mounts to a halt, throwing dirt and raising dust, Lisa stood up. Dan leapt from his saddle and ran toward his daughter, taking her into his arms. She quickly filled him in on what had happened, telling him how U.S. Marshal Ben Bryce had killed the three outlaws, saving her from certain death.

While Mills went to aid Donna Stack, Lisa led her father to the federal man. She told Dan Washburn, "We've got to get him to Dr. Townsend as soon as possible. His wound must be sewn up to stop the bleeding."

Leaving Donna Stack's side and hurrying to Lisa, Ned Mills put in, "I think perhaps you should be worrying about yourself. You've had a terrible shock." Then he took the young woman in his arms, telling her, "I was beside myself when Bob and Dave told us you had been kidnapped. I'm so glad you're safe, darling."

Lisa pulled herself free of the deputy's embrace and smiled at the federal man. "If it hadn't been for Marshal Bryce, I wouldn't be safe."

It was nearing midday when U.S. Marshal Ben Bryce was carried into Dr. John Townsend's office by Raton's two lawmen. The silver-haired physician stitched up Bryce's wound, then bandaged it. When he was finished, he placed his instruments on a counter behind the table where the federal man lay, then stood over him.

Looking down at Bryce, the doctor's eyes twinkled with good humor as he declared, "Son, I know how you young bucks are. You think you're real tough and can bounce back from a gunshot wound immediately. Do I have your attention?"

Bryce looked him square in the eye, a grin tugging at the corner of his mouth. "Yes, sir."

"Good," Townsend declared authoritatively. "Now, I want you flat on your back for a full day. By late tomorrow you can sit up in bed some, and day after tomorrow you can begin walking around the room a little. I'll be in and out, but I'll try to wait on you as much as I can." The physician paused, then added, "Incidentally, you won't be able to do any riding for a while. And I mean *no* riding. Just even try climbing onto a horse, and you'll rip open your wound."

"Tell you what, Doc," spoke up Dan Washburn. "Marshal Bryce can come to our house and stay for the next few days while he's recuperating. We have two extra bedrooms since the boys got married and moved out, and he's welcome to stay in one of them. Darlene and Lisa can take care of him."

The federal man gazed at Dan Washburn. "I hate putting you to so much trouble, Marshal."

"Nonsense," Dan retorted. "It's the least we can do to thank you for saving Lisa's life."

Bryce looked from father to daughter. "Are you sure about this? Maybe you should ask Mrs. Washburn first."

"We both know what Mother will say, Marshal," the

blond beauty replied. "She has a soft spot for men who wear a badge. She's married to one, after all."

Across the room, Ned Mills's face was the picture of gloom as he stared at Lisa Washburn. A strange look entered the young blonde's eyes whenever she looked at Ben Bryce—a look that was never there when she looked at the deputy.

The federal man was taken back to the Washburn house in the family buckboard, and he was soon settled in. Lying in his bed, he watched Lisa Washburn as she fussed with the blanket, and when he caught her eye, he smiled at her and said, "I can see that you're going to be a dedicated nurse."

"You're right," Lisa agreed, smiling back. "I owe you my life, Marshal Bryce, therefore I'm going to see that you get well as soon as possible."

Darlene entered the room carrying a pitcher of water and a glass and put in cheerfully, "We're *both* going to see that you get well as soon as possible." Setting the pitcher and the glass on the bedstand, she added, "One of us will be within earshot at all times. When you need us, just call out."

Bryce laughed. "You two could spoil a fella so bad he might not want to get well."

Lisa peered at him. "Seems to me, Marshal, that you're not the type of man who could bear lying around very long."

Gazing intently at Lisa, Bryce responded softly, "I guess you're right, but with a gorgeous young woman like you to feast my eyes on every day, it sure would be tempting to play sick for a while."

The young blonde blushed and looked away, catching her mother's eye. Darlene looked at her daughter for a long moment, then smiled knowingly.

Footsteps sounded from the hallway, and a moment later Ned Mills entered the room, hat in hand, with the marshal behind him. "I, uh, just came by to see how our patient is doing."

"He's doing just fine, Ned," replied Darlene. "Lisa and I are going to take very good care of him."

The deputy nodded, and his voice was almost curt as he remarked, "Good. I certainly hope the marshal gets well and he's able to be on his way very soon."

He then stepped over to Lisa and took hold of her hand. "And how are you doing, darling? Have you recovered from your ordeal?"

Slipping her hand from Ned's, Lisa replied, "I'll be fine."

The deputy's face grew red as jealousy crawled through him like a fever. His jaw muscles working, he put his arm around the young woman's shoulder and suggested, "Why don't you go lie down for a while? You probably should rest after going through such a horrible experience."

Lisa shrugged off his arm and moved beside her mother, irritation showing in her eyes. "I'll be fine, Ned. You don't have to fuss so. As a matter of fact, I think Mother and I should leave you men to visit while we attend to our chores."

"No time for visiting right now," spoke up Dan Washburn. "Ned and I have things to do at the office. Besides, I think Marshal Bryce is the one who needs to get some rest."

The room was soon emptied, and U.S. Marshal Ben Bryce lay on his back, staring up at the ceiling. *I wonder,* he asked himself, *what such a charming and beautiful woman as Lisa Washburn can see in a guy like Ned Mills.* Smiling, he then thought, *Of course, when I think about it, she doesn't seem to see much in him at all.*

That evening after everyone had eaten, the Washburns spent some time in Ben Bryce's room, learning more about their houseguest.

The young federal marshal revealed that he, Benjamin Lloyd Bryce, had been born in southern Arizona thirty-two years before. First serving as Tucson's deputy marshal for three years, he had then been town marshal for six years before resigning to become a federal marshal. Since pinning on the government badge a year and a half ago, he had been working out of the El Paso office. He went on to explain how he had pursued the three killers for two weeks and finally ended up chasing them through Raton.

When Bryce began to show signs of weariness, Darlene suggested they let him get to sleep, and bidding him good-night, they left the room. As the Washburns walked along the hallway, Lisa turned to her parents and said, "Actually, I think everything that's happened today has finally caught up with me. I'm ready for bed, too." Standing on her tiptoes, she kissed her father on his cheek, then kissed her mother. "Good night," she said, yawning.

"Good night, honey," Dan responded. "Sweet dreams."

When Lisa was out of earshot, Dan remarked to his wife, "Our daughter definitely has eyes for young Bryce."

"She certainly does," agreed Darlene.

"Do you suppose Ben is married?" asked Dan.

Darlene was thoughtful for a moment, then answered, "Seems to me if he were, he would have mentioned having a wife at one point this evening. Besides, he seems to be as attracted to Lisa as she is to him." She sighed. "But it probably doesn't matter. After all, he won't be here very long."

Chapter Four

Two days after U.S. Marshal Ben Bryce had been shot, Dr. John Townsend came to the Washburn house to check on his patient. Examining the wound, the physician was pleased with Bryce's progress, and while he rebandaged the lawman he advised him that he was healing nicely. Townsend prepared to leave, and closing up his black bag, he asked Bryce, "Did you sit up at all yesterday?"

"Yes, sir. For about three hours."

"Good. Today you should walk around the room a little, then tomorrow a little more, and increase your time out of bed each day. You're recovering very quickly—so quickly that I should be able to remove the stitches in another four or five days. But I want to remind you that it'll be at least two weeks after that before you can do any lengthy riding."

Turning to Lisa and Darlene Washburn, who stood watching solicitously, Townsend told them, "You ladies are doing an excellent job of taking care of this man." He grinned, adding, "As a matter of fact, since you've nursed him as well as you have, you've not left much for me to do. So that being the case, I may as well go attend to those patients who really need me."

Laughing, Darlene Washburn escorted the physician to the door. When they had gone, Bryce told Lisa again how much he appreciated the kindness and hospitality the family was showing him. "Especially you, Lisa. You're spending a considerable amount of your time tending to my needs."

"Oh, I don't mind," she assured him. "Quite to the contrary. You see—"

Lisa was interrupted by the sudden appearance of Ned Mills. Manifesting concern for Bryce, Mills pulled a chair beside the bed and began talking to the lawman about what were essentially trivial matters. Bryce saw through the deputy's façade, but he did not let on. It was quite evident that Mills was possessive of Lisa, pointedly using endearing terms while addressing her in Bryce's presence to impress the federal man that there was something between them. The young marshal could plainly see that Mills resented Lisa's caring for him.

When the deputy finally left, Lisa pushed the chair back to the window and announced, "All right, Marshal Bryce, it's time for you to follow doctor's orders and take a little walk."

Putting on a robe borrowed from Dan Washburn, Ben Bryce got out of bed assisted by Lisa. He walked slowly around the room on slightly unsteady feet while the blonde sat in the chair, watching him intently. Lisa's face disclosed that she was captivated by the ruggedly handsome lawman. "You're standing quite straight for a man who has stitches in his side," she remarked, smiling.

The U.S. marshal chuckled. "You know why, don't you? It's the expert care I've been getting."

Lisa nodded in agreement. "Yes, Mother is an expert, all right. She's nursed Dad through more than one bullet wound."

Coming over to the chair, Bryce stood looking down at Lisa. "With all due respect to your mother," he told her, "I was referring to you."

"Why, thank you, Marshal Bryce," Lisa responded coyly. "That's the nicest compliment I've ever had."

The lawman started circumnavigating the room again, and Lisa watched his progress, her eyes never leaving him. She asked him a few questions about life as a federal marshal, then, clearing her throat, she inquired in a casual voice, "Are you married?"

The lawman grinned crookedly. "Nope."

Lisa's face reflected her relief. She had opened her mouth to say something else, when Bryce declared, "You're probably wondering if there's something wrong with me."

"Why would I do that?"

He shrugged. "I *am* thirty-two. Most men are long married by my age."

"Well, I—"

"The reason I've never married, Lisa," he continued levelly, "is that I simply haven't found the right woman —one who's eager to marry a man who wears a badge. Especially a traveling federal marshal." He smiled, adding, "That's what I need—a woman who'll love me enough to marry me in spite of the piece of metal that's usually pinned on my chest."

Without commenting, Lisa stood up and advised, "I think that's enough exercise for today, Marshal. Come on. I'll help you get back into bed." When her patient was settled once more, Lisa suggested, "You should try and sleep a while. I'll look in on you later."

Bryce nodded silently and watched her walk toward the door. When she was about to leave the room, he murmured, "Of course, it wouldn't hurt if she was good-looking, too."

Lisa paused and looked over her shoulder, her face puzzled.

"I was just saying that if I found a woman like that, it wouldn't hurt if she was good-looking besides."

"Oh. No, I guess it wouldn't hurt at all, would it?" She gave him a distracted smile, then left.

On Raton's main street later that day, lovely dark-eyed Dolores Domingo emerged from the general store just as Manuel Lucero came down the street in his wagon. When Manuel saw her, he pulled rein and stopped in front of her.

Grinning happily, Manuel declared, "Hello, Dolores. It is a beautiful day, is it not?"

"Hello, Mr. Lucero." She smiled in return, stepping to the edge of the boardwalk. "Are . . . are you heading for Santa Fe now?"

"That is correct. I am very excited to bring my Tony home."

A shadow of sadness clouded Dolores's beautiful eyes. "I never received a reply from Tony, Mr. Lucero. Do you know if he got my letter telling him that I am going to marry Juan on November first?"

"Yes, he did, Dolores. He wrote me that he did not answer you because he did not know what to say. I believe you can understand that."

Nodding slowly, she replied, "Yes. Yes, I do, Mr. Lucero. I just hope Tony understands why I let myself fall in love with Juan. When I promised Tony I would wait for him, I did not realize how long ten years would be." She looked down for a moment, then murmured, "Of course, I did not know that he would be getting out so soon."

"I will not say that the news did not hit my son very hard, Dolores," Manuel admitted, "but Tony is a sensible boy. I am sure he does not blame you."

"I hope not," she responded with trembling lips.

Dolores Domingo had been shocked when she learned that Tony Lucero was going to be released from prison five years sooner than had been expected. Since then, she had spent many sleepless nights, wondering if she had been too hasty in her decision to marry Juan Gomez. Secretly agonizing over her dilemma, she told herself that she had no choice; she had to abide by her promise to Juan. Besides, he was a good man, and she had no doubt that he would make a good husband.

"Tony still loves you, Dolores," Manuel added, "and I know he wants you to be happy. If you can be happy with Juan, Tony will want that for you."

Dolores was fighting to keep from crying when she looked across the street and saw Juan coming out of the bank. The big husky Mexican spotted her and crossed toward her, his muscles straining against his shirt as he walked. He made his living doing odd jobs for ranchers and farmers around Raton, and his years of laboring had made him as hard as a rock and as strong as a bull ox. A quiet man, he could get mean when riled.

There was a frown on Juan's face as he approached Dolores. Looking into her eyes, he asked, "You seem troubled. Is something wrong?"

"No," she responded, trying to cover the strain she was feeling. "Mr. Lucero is on his way to pick up his son at the prison, and I was telling him that I am pleased for them both that Tony will have his freedom."

"Your eyes tell me that you are unhappy, Dolores," insisted Juan.

"Not unhappy," she insisted, shaking her head. "It is just that I do not know what I will say to Tony when he returns. We were engaged, after all."

Looking at Manuel, Juan asked, "Do you think Tony will cause trouble?"

"No," replied Manuel, his voice very certain. "Tony has had enough trouble in his life. You need not concern yourself over that."

Manuel then excused himself and drove off. After watching him go, the husky Mexican put his hands on Dolores's shoulders and said, "I think it would be best if we were already married before Tony arrives home."

But Dolores shook her head. Taking hold of his arm, she told Juan, "I want our wedding to be just as we have planned it. If we move up the date, we will not have time to prepare properly. Believe me, there will be no trouble from Tony. He is not a violent person when he is sober, and he has sworn never to drink again."

Giving in, Juan Gomez took Dolores by the hand and walked her home.

Toward dusk Marshal Dan Washburn and his deputy heard sudden gunfire outside, accompanied by hoarse laughter. Dan was out the door of his office in a flash, with Ned Mills on his heels. In the middle of the street, six cowhands from the nearby Bar X ranch were terrorizing an old man, making him dance as they fired into the ground near his feet. Townspeople lined the boardwalks on both sides of the street, watching in horror as the bullets barely missed the elderly man.

The marshal's eyes turned the color of slate, and anger darkened his face. Less than two weeks before, these same troublemakers had come into Raton, gotten tanked up on whiskey at the Lucky Dog Saloon, then started shooting up the town. At that time Washburn had ordered them to get out and never return. Yet here they were again, and it was evident that they had been drinking—and now, with their bellies full of whiskey, they were ready for what they considered fun.

Thundering onto the scene, Dan Washburn bellowed, "All right, that's enough!"

The shooting ceased slowly as one by one the six cowhands held their fire, then grinned insolently at the marshal, their eyes bloodshot and bleary. The afternoon breeze blew the clouds of gunsmoke away, and their leader, a tall, gangly man named Bart Ohms, waggled his head and leered at Dan. His tongue thick from the effects of the alcohol, he slurred, "Hey, Marshal, we don't want no trouble. We was just havin' a little fun."

Waiting until the elderly man had hobbled over to the boardwalk and the safety of the crowd, Dan then glared at the cowboy and snapped, "I told you to stay out of this town, Ohms!"

The drunken cowboy held his gun loosely at his side and pouted. "Now, Marshal, that ain't very neighborly."

Ignoring the statement, Dan Washburn demanded, "Did you get your whiskey at the Lucky Dog?"

"Yeah. So what?"

The marshal looked toward the saloon. Dexter Finn was standing in the doorway, holding the batwings open and fixing the marshal with wary, piercing eyes. The lawman looked back at Ohms and growled, "I'm going to give you a choice, mister—and that includes your five pals. You can each pay a fine of fifty dollars for disturbing the peace, or you can sit it out for thirty days in my jail. Which will it be?"

All six men erupted with a babel of angry words, featured among which were cries of "Fifty dollars! That's almost a month's pay!" Bart Ohms ran his blurred gaze over the reddened faces of his five friends, then looked back at the lawman and licked his lips. "Well, Marshal, I guess the fact is ain't none of us in no condition to buck the likes of you. So I guess we'd best pay the fine." He sneered, adding, "I guess it's lucky we just got paid—otherwise we'd all be off to jail and your one-horse town'd be out some easy revenue."

While the crowd looked on, Marshal Dan Washburn collected the money from each Bar X man. Determined that these cowhands would never return to Raton, the lawman warned Ohms, "If you or any of your Bar X troublemakers so much as step foot in my town again, I'll arrest you the minute I see you and you'll do ninety days in jail. You got that?"

Ohms bristled. "Now, look here, Washburn! You can't—"

"Oh, can't I?" the marshal cut in. "You just try me!" Gesturing toward their mounts, still tied in front of the saloon, he ordered, "Now, find your saddles and get out of my sight . . . for good!"

Like whipped dogs, the six men did as they were told,

shambling to their mounts, then riding out of town as fast as their horses could carry them.

Dan Washburn glanced over at Dexter Finn. His fists doubled in rage, the burly saloonkeeper stomped off the boardwalk and stormed across the street. Thrusting his face within inches of the marshal's, he spat, "You got no call to run them out of town for good, Washburn! The Bar X ranch drops a lot of money in my till! You're costing me plenty by being so rotten bullheaded! Now, I demand—"

"You're not in a position to demand anything, Finn!" retorted Washburn angrily.

"Now, look!" exploded the owner of the Lucky Dog. "You've run off my customers time and time again, and I'm sick of it. I'm not putting up with it anymore!"

"And just what do you plan to do?" queried Washburn.

Fuming, Finn snarled, "I don't know, but I'll think of something."

"I told you a few days ago what your alternatives are, Finn," the marshal said levelly.

Finn's jaw jutted angrily. "Yeah," he grunted, opening and closing his powerful fists, "but maybe there are some alternatives you haven't thought of."

Washburn's face stiffened and his eyes narrowed. "Just what do you mean by that?"

Finn wheeled and headed for his saloon.

"I asked you a question!" shouted Washburn.

"Come up with your own answer!" Finn yelled sharply over his shoulder, then disappeared through the doors of his saloon.

Dan Washburn stared at the swinging doors for a long moment, considering going after Finn and demanding a response. Then, deciding it best to control his own hot temper, he turned and headed back to the office.

At seven o'clock that evening a town meeting was held at the town hall, presided over by Weston DeRose.

The marshal stood before the people, and reminding them of Leo Dunn's horrid death, he told them it was time Raton started using a gallows to execute criminals, explaining how quick and certain death was when a gallows was used.

Weston DeRose then spoke up and announced, "Folks, I will pay for the construction of the gallows, provided it is erected in plain sight. I think everybody ought to be able to see it whenever they come or go from this town, for I feel strongly that its very presence could have an effect on lawbreakers and troublemakers."

The people readily agreed, and it was decided that the gallows would be built on a knoll just beyond the north end of Main Street. With that settled, DeRose looked over at Abe Washburn, who was sitting in the front row. "Abe," he said, "you're our best carpenter. You want the job?"

"Sure," consented the huge man. "I'll get to it as soon as possible."

"Any idea how long that will be?"

Abe scratched his head. "Well, let me think. I'll be busy with other work for about six or seven weeks before I'll be able to begin. If that's all right . . . "

"I think it will be," DeRose replied. Then he smiled. "Let's hope we won't need to execute anybody for at least that long."

Ben Bryce was sitting in the parlor reading a book when Dan, Darlene, and Lisa Washburn returned home after the town meeting. As they seated themselves, the U.S. marshal asked, "So how'd it go?"

"Just fine," replied Dan. "The idea of a gallows was heartily approved. My brother, Abe, is going to build it."

"Wise move," commented Bryce. Then he ran his gaze over his hosts' faces and told them, "I want to thank you again for your kind hospitality and for nursing me back to health. Tomorrow I'll be moving to the Raton Hotel so you people can get your lives back to normal."

Lisa quickly spoke up, "Marshal Bryce, it isn't necessary that you move to the hotel."

The federal man smiled. "Thanks, but I don't want to wear out my welcome, Lisa."

"You could never do that," the blonde replied with feeling. "Besides, since you're only going to be here a few more weeks, we'd like you to continue to stay with us." She looked at her parents for confirmation, asking, "Isn't that right?"

Both Dan and Darlene agreed in unison. "And I might add," Raton's marshal added, "that it's a privilege to have you in our home."

Darlene laughed. "I'd say you'll have to give in, Marshal."

"I'd say you're right, ma'am," Bryce rejoined. He looked at Lisa, and it was clear from her eyes that something was bothering her. The federal man found himself wishing he would not have to leave the beautiful blonde, but he covered his feelings.

After chatting a while longer, Dan and Darlene agreed it was time for bed, and Lisa remarked that she, too, was tired. Bryce told them he wanted to sit up for a while and read some more of the book, and after bidding each other good-night, the Washburns retired.

About an hour later, Bryce marked his place in the book and laid it down. He stood up, yawned, and rubbed his eyes. Dousing the lamp, he waited until his eyes had adjusted slightly to the dark, then made his way across the parlor and headed down the hallway. A crack of yellow light showed under Lisa's door, and he wondered if she was lying in bed reading. He was just about to open his door when Lisa came out of her room and they collided.

"Whoops!" she said as the impact knocked her off balance.

Ben Bryce reached out quickly and grabbed her to keep her from falling. "Sorry," he murmured, holding her with his strong hands. "I didn't hear you coming."

Clad in a soft nightgown, her long blond hair lying on her shoulders, Lisa smelled of lilacs, and Bryce wondered if it was her soap or perhaps a sachet. She made no move to release herself from his grip, and their eyes met in the faint light that came from her room. Suddenly her beauty, her closeness, and her sweet scent were too much for the young lawman. Before he knew it, he was kissing her—and Lisa was yielding quite willingly. He abruptly broke off the kiss and looked away from her. "I . . . I'm sorry, Lisa," he apologized. "I shouldn't have taken advantage of you like that."

Lisa Washburn's eyes danced with delight. "I wouldn't say you took advantage of me, Marshal," she rejoined in a slightly husky voice.

"But I know you belong to Ned Mills."

"Ned Mills?" she gasped incredulously. "What makes you think I belong to him?"

"Well . . . you know . . . he comes around here a lot. And he calls you by some pretty endearing terms. I presumed—"

Staying close to him, Lisa cut in, "There is nothing between Ned and me. The feelings he professes are all on his part. I assure you, I have no romantic inclinations toward Ned Mills whatsoever. My feelings toward him are those of a sister."

Bryce was pleased, but he insisted, "I still had no right to kiss you."

Moving closer and lifting her face toward his, Lisa said softly, "You have a right to kiss me if I give you that right." Their lips came together again, and when the kiss was finished, they looked into each other's eyes for a long moment.

"I wish you didn't have to go away," she murmured.

Grinning, Bryce responded, "I'm starting to wish the

same thing myself." He reluctantly released her and was about to enter his room when he turned back and looked at her. "Good night, Lisa," he whispered.

"Good night . . . Ben," she whispered back.

Chapter Five

It was just after ten o'clock the following Saturday morning when Manuel Lucero's wagon rattled into Raton with Manuel's handsome son, Tony, riding beside his father.

The twenty-seven-year-old Tony stared straight ahead, an impenetrable look on his finely chiseled face. He could feel the harsh glares that were sent his way by many of the people they passed, and he refused to acknowledge them. A large hat partially shielded his face, covering his black wavy hair, and a bead of sweat glistened on his thin mustache. Of average height, Tony Lucero had gotten even slimmer than usual since his incarceration.

Manuel lifted a hand to wave at various passersby, but the presence of his ex-convict son kept the people from waving back. No one seemed glad to see Tony Lucero return to Raton.

Manuel hauled up in front of Willows's Clothing Store and set the brake. "What are you doing, Papa?" queried Tony.

"We've got to get you some new clothes, son," explained the older Lucero, smiling. "Since you are starting life anew, you should have some new clothes to do so in."

"I agree that I need new clothes, Papa," responded the handsome young Mexican, "but I am not sure that changing my clothes will change the feelings of the citizens of Raton. Maybe I have made a mistake in coming back here. Perhaps the best thing is for me to go elsewhere and start my life over."

"Nonsense," retorted Manuel as he stepped down from the wagon seat. "You have paid your debt to society. You can walk the streets of Raton with your head held high. This is your home, Tony. You have as much right to live here as anyone else does."

Entering the shop, father and son found there were no other customers in the store. Proprietor Edgar Willows, a small, thin man of fifty, looked up from where he stood behind the counter, an automatic welcoming smile on his lips. Upon seeing Tony Lucero's face, his smile vanished.

"Good morning, Mr. Willows," Manuel said cheerfully. "As you see, my son is home now, and we need to get him some new clothes. I have been saving money for this occasion." Pulling a wad of green bills from a pocket, he instructed, "I wish to purchase three shirts, three pairs of pants, some long underwear, three pairs of socks, and a new pair of boots."

"Of course," Willows responded, looking coldly at Tony. "Take a look around. When you find what you want, bring the items here to the counter."

Surprise showed on Manuel's swarthy face. "But Mr. Willows, is it not your custom to show us what you have? To guide us in our purchase?"

Throwing another frosty glance at young Lucero, then looking at Manuel but not quite meeting his gaze, Willows replied, "Well, yes. But then, I haven't had convicts come into my store before."

Manuel's face darkened with anger. "My son is no longer a convict, Mr. Willows," he muttered thickly. "He has been paroled after paying for his misdeed. Surely you know that the prison officials released him long before his sentence was complete because he had been such a model prisoner." He shook his head. "I cannot believe that you—"

Tony put a gentle yet firm hand on his father's shoulder. Quietly he said, "Papa, do not become angry with Mr. Willows. I did break the law, and I have been a convict for five years. He has a right to dislike me if he chooses." Then to Willows he remarked, "If you would rather we did not patronize your store, I can get clothing somewhere else."

Edgar Willows looked uncomfortable and nervously cleared his throat. "Oh, no, Tony. Of course not. It's just that . . . well, you know—"

"Just that *what*?" demanded Manuel, growing angrier. "My boy is contaminating your place, is that it?"

Willows cleared his throat again. "Of course not. It's just that, well, Raton is a nice respectable town, and—"

"It is my desire to regain my respectability, Mr. Willows," cut in young Lucero. "I did wrong, and I know it. All I ask of the people here is that they give me a chance to prove that I can be a good citizen once again, and that I can be an asset to the town. Would you at least give me that chance?"

The proprietor's face tinted. Lowering his head, he gazed at Tony and murmured, "Sure, kid. Sure. I'm sorry I was rude to you. Come on. Let's see what we've got that'll fit you."

Manuel Lucero walked stiffly beside his son, clearly fighting hard to squelch his anger as Willows took them through the store and helped Tony pick out the things that he needed. Twenty minutes later, their purchases wrapped in paper and tied with string, the two Mexicans headed out of the shop. Just as they reached the door, in came Herman Franks, the Raton Community Bank's new president. A short, stout man of fifty-five with an ample belly, Franks had been the bank's vice president until George Todd was murdered by Leo Dunn. Franks was also on the town council.

When Manuel Lucero and his son saw Franks enter

the store, they braced themselves, expecting more antagonism. They were pleasantly surprised when the stout banker smiled, extended his hand to the ex-convict, and exclaimed, "Tony! Welcome home! You're a little thinner than when I saw you last, but other than that, you look just the same—and as handsome as ever."

Tony pumped Franks's hand, smiling warmly in return. "It is good to see you again, Mr. Franks. Papa tells me you are president of the bank now."

"Yes," Franks sighed, nodding slowly. "Too bad my promotion came about under such tragic circumstances."

"I was very sorry to hear about that," responded young Lucero.

Manuel turned and gave Edgar Willows a smug look, as if to say, *See there! Everybody in Raton does not treat my son as if he were dirt!*

The banker asked Tony, "Are you planning to stay in Raton?"

"Yes, sir."

"What are you going to do for a living?"

"He'll find a job, Mr. Franks," Manuel answered for him. "Tony is a hard worker, and he is good at whatever he tries. We are aware that his having been in prison will make it more difficult to find someone who will hire him, but my boy will do all right. You can bet on it."

"I'm sure he will, Manuel," agreed Franks with a grin. Then to Tony he offered, "Let me know if there's anything I can do for you."

Father and son both thanked the banker, then left the store. As they stepped onto the boardwalk, they were surprised to see that a crowd had gathered. They laid the packages in the bed of their wagon under the watchful eyes of their fellow citizens, some of whom were obviously merely curious—but others of whom were openly hostile.

"Hey, jailbird!" came a young male voice from the midst of the throng. "Who you gonna stab this time?"

Laughter followed, along with some jeers.

"Yeah!" called out another. "Remind me to leave town when you get drunk!"

Manuel's back stiffened. Tony saw the fire in his father's eyes and quickly said in a low voice, "Do not let them anger you, Papa. Let's just get in the wagon and drive home."

A small boy who stood next to his mother pointed at Tony and spoke up for all to hear, "Is that him, Mommy? Is that the man you said was real bad?"

The young woman's face reddened. She threw Tony a quick glance, seized the boy's hand, and quickly dragged him away.

Then a young man in his early twenties stepped close to Tony and announced harshly, "You're a bad man, all right. Why did you have to come back here anyway, Lucero? We don't want you!"

Manuel glared at the young man and started for him, but Tony gripped him by the arms and said calmly, "Come on, Papa. Get in the wagon, and let's go home."

While his son held him fast, the older Lucero eyed the young man and told him heatedly, "You do not own this town, Harold! Tony has as much right to live here as you do! Why do you have to be so hateful?"

Before Harold Bentley could respond, Tony told the crowd calmly, "I have not forgotten that I got drunk and stabbed Dominic Ortega, so I do not expect you people to forget it. But if my good behavior behind the penitentiary walls proved my good intentions to the prison officials—giving them enough faith in me to parole me five years early—I ask that you also let me prove to you my desire to live peacefully."

Dan Washburn and Ned Mills suddenly approached the crowd, and as they did, someone asked loudly, "What about the threat you made to our marshal, Tony?"

"I made that remark in the heat of anger. But that is something I will discuss with the marshal later," young

Lucero answered with complete self-possession. "Right now I just want to go home and see my mother and my sisters."

The Luceros started to climb into their buckboard when Abe Washburn stepped beside the young Mexican. Holding on to the side of the wagon, he remarked, "I heard the ruckus from my shop and came to see what it was all about. Tony, I didn't hear all that went on out here, but I did hear you say that you want the chance to prove yourself to our town."

"That is correct, Mr. Washburn," confirmed Tony, then he settled in the seat and picked up the reins.

"I believe you, son," Abe said kindly. "I take it you need a job."

"I sure do, sir."

"Well, I tell you what. I believe you when you say you mean my brother no harm, and my business is doing so good that I need a helper. You interested?"

Tony flashed the big blacksmith a wide grin. "Yes, sir!"

Clapping the young man on the shoulder, Abe declared, "Good! If you're willing to work hard—put in some long hours—I'll pay you well. Can you start immediately?"

"How about first thing Monday morning?"

Nodding, Abe agreed, "See you at seven."

Manuel Lucero's eyes filled with tears as he smiled at the blacksmith. "This is a most decent thing to do for us, Mr. Washburn, and I cannot thank you enough for your kindness."

"Nor I," added Tony. With that, he grinned again, then flicked the reins and drove away.

As Manuel and his son headed up Main Street toward their home just outside the edge of town, Tony abruptly stated, "Papa, I want to stop at Flora Domingo's house and see Dolores."

Manuel's brow puckered. "You mean right now, son?"

"Yes."

Manuel lifted his battered old hat, scratched his head nervously, then suggested, "Maybe that would not be the best thing to do, son. Why don't you wait until you've been home a day or two. Let it be a casual meeting. It is really not—"

"I have to see her, Papa," cut in Tony.

"Tony, listen to me," argued the senior Lucero. "Juan Gomez will probably be there, and like everyone else, he is also probably expecting trouble from you over Dolores. He might even start something out of fear or jealousy. You are an ex-convict, and any trouble could ruin everything for you. Mr. Washburn has been very kind to give you a job. Please do not jeopardize it by looking for trouble."

Tony looked at his father from the corner of his eye and smiled solicitously. "Papa, do not worry. I am not going to cause any trouble, and I am not going to get into any trouble. I just want to see Dolores for a few minutes—after all, it has been five years since I have seen her. I just want her to know that I still love her, but that I want her to be happy. I could not put it in a letter, but I can say it to her in person. I want her to know that I wish her well."

When they reached Flora Domingo's house, Manuel Lucero sat in the wagon as his son mounted the porch and knocked on the door. The door opened, revealing the slender form of Flora Domingo, a woman in her late forties. Her eyes showed a hint of fear at the sight of Tony Lucero standing before her.

With a pleasant tone in his voice Tony smiled and said, "Good morning, Mrs. Domingo. You are looking well. Is Dolores here?"

Flora swallowed hard, keeping her eyes riveted on young Lucero's face, and replied shakily, "Y-yes, she is here, Tony, but she has a guest right now—the . . . ah . . . the man she is going to marry. They are sitting on the back porch."

Seeing the trepidation in Flora's eyes, Tony advised, "I assure you, Mrs. Domingo, I mean no harm to Dolores nor to Juan Gomez. I only ask for a few minutes of her time."

Nodding, Flora gestured toward the corner of the house and said, "You know the way."

Tony thanked her and headed around the house, giving his father a brief glance over his shoulder.

As he rounded the back corner of the house, Tony found Dolores and Juan sitting together on a bench, their backs against the wall of the house.

Dolores saw him first. "Tony!" she gasped, tensing up.

The husky Mexican leapt to his feet, bristling.

Drawing near, Tony smiled and told the beautiful young woman, "I just got into town, Dolores. I am sure you have been dreading the moment we would first see each other again, so I wanted to get it over with. Your aunt told me Juan was here, so I thought I would come back and take care of everything that I wish to tell you both all at once."

Dolores stood up slowly as Tony looked at Juan and told him, "I want you to know that I have no intention of causing you trouble. I want Dolores to have a happy and wonderful life, and if she is in love with you and can find happiness as your wife, this is what I want." Turning to Dolores, he choked slightly with emotion as he added, "I cannot blame you for finding someone else, Dolores. You are young and very beautiful, and ten years would have been a very long time to wait for me."

Juan and Dolores looked at each other in amazement, clearly surprised by Tony's attitude.

Stepping closer to the couple, Tony looked lovingly at the dark-haired beauty and said with difficulty, "I must tell you, Dolores, that I love you more than any other man could ever love you. But since you are engaged to Juan, I will stay out of your life." Facing Juan, he admitted, "I envy you, and I cannot blame you for falling in love with Dolores. She is the most wonderful girl that

God ever made. You are most fortunate to have her love. All I ask is that you make her happy and always treat her kindly."

Juan gave Tony an understanding smile. His voice was slightly constricted as he replied, "I promise you I will do that, Lucero."

Tony glanced at Dolores, and it was clear that his words had touched her deeply. He gave her another loving smile, then walked back around the corner of the house and returned to his wagon. After giving his father a reassuring look, he flicked the reins and they drove off.

Dolores's body began trembling, and Juan folded her into his powerful arms, holding her tight. They listened silently to the sound of the retreating wagon until it finally died away. Then, pulling his head back slightly to see her face, he looked deep into her eyes and asked softly, "You are still in love with him, aren't you?"

The young woman protested, "No, Juan, I . . . I am in love with you. Truly I am." She put her hand to her head and looked away. "I do not feel well. I need to go in the house and lie down."

Juan released her, and Dolores turned toward the door of the house. Assuring Juan that she would be all right if she could rest for a while, the young woman hurried to her room. Once there, she flung herself on the bed and sobbed.

Moments later Flora Domingo entered the room, closing the door behind her. Embracing her niece, she murmured, "There, there, child. I know how upsetting this must be for you."

"Oh, Aunt Flora," Dolores sniffed, "I am so confused. I thought I was over Tony . . . until I saw him. Now I know I am still deeply in love with him. But what can I do? I do not want to hurt Juan."

Flora stroked her niece's long black hair as Dolores wept softly. With compassion in her voice Flora said, "I cannot tell you what to do, my dear. This is a decision that only you can make. You will just have to follow the dictates of your heart."

After a few minutes Dolores regained her composure. She stood up and straightened her dress, then wiped her tear-streaked face. Flora gave her another quick hug, then stated, "I will leave you to speak with Juan alone. This is a matter that is between the two of you, and you do not need to feel constrained by my presence." So saying, Flora went to her room.

When Dolores emerged from her room, she saw Juan waiting in the kitchen. She went to him and he rose from the chair, his black eyes staring piercingly at her. Taking her hand, he insisted, "Dolores, you must tell me the truth. Are you still in love with Tony?"

A sick feeling crawled through Dolores Domingo. She looked at the floor, not wanting to answer.

Still tenderly holding Dolores's hand, Juan pressed for a reply. "You told me a little while ago that you love me. But after seeing how you reacted to Tony Lucero, I believe what you feel for me is secondary to what you feel for him. If I am wrong—and I pray that I am—I want you to look me straight in the eye and tell me so."

Dolores's head came up slowly. With extreme difficulty she met his probing gaze and murmured, "I cannot lie to you, Juan. You must believe that I thought I was completely over Tony. When I pledged my love to you, I meant it. It was not until he appeared today that I realized I still love him. The old flame in my heart came alive the moment I saw him. I . . . I am sorry, Juan. I do not want to hurt you."

Juan dropped her hand and looked away from her. "What if he ends up going back to prison?" he challenged. "What then? Will you expect me to take you back?"

Dolores's lips quivered as she responded, "Tony will not go back to prison, Juan. I know it."

"How do you know it?" he demanded. "I have heard much about the vengeance he feels toward Marshal

Washburn. When he exacts that vengeance, he will go back to prison. Can you not see that you are setting yourself up for more heartache like you knew when he went to prison the first time?"

Defending the man she loved, Dolores insisted, "Tony will not take vengeance on the marshal, Juan. It has been five long years since he threatened him, and I am sure he has forgotten it by now."

Heartbreak and anger comingled in Juan Gomez's face. His voice cutting, he snapped, "Go ahead and throw your life away on that worthless criminal, Dolores! But I am telling you that one day you will wish you had married me." With that he whirled and stormed out of the house, slamming the door hard.

Flora Domingo came rushing into the kitchen, taking Dolores in her arms while the young woman wept. After finally composing herself, Dolores told her aunt all that was in her heart. Some minutes later she stood up, a resolute expression on her face. "I must go to Tony. I have to tell him that I still love him."

Throwing on a light shawl, Dolores hurried to the small barn behind the house and saddled her horse. She led the animal beside the back door, calling out that she would return shortly. Then she mounted up and rode toward the Lucero house two miles east of town.

Carmen Lucero was a short, plump woman with silver streaks in her long dark hair, which she wore in a bun on the back of her head. A bundle of energy, after welcoming her son home with tears of joy, she returned to the kitchen, bustling around with her two daughters —fourteen-year-old Consuelo and twelve-year-old Lita —in preparing a homecoming feast.

Carmen was standing by the window, making tortillas, when she spotted a rider galloping up the road. She was surprised to see the horse turn into the Lucero yard —and her surprise turned to shock when she recognized Dolores Domingo. She gasped, then called out

Dolores's name and hurried from the house. Dolores slid from the saddle and embraced the older woman. At the same moment Tony came out of the house, having heard his mother shout Dolores's name.

Dolores let go of Carmen and walked slowly toward Tony. He stepped off the porch and stood looking at her with speculation.

The young woman's eyes were moist as she stammered, "Tony, I . . . I . . . "

"Yes, Dolores?"

Rushing to him, Dolores flung her arms around him and cried, "Oh, Tony, I had to come to you! I love you, my darling! I love you!"

Young Lucero embraced her and held her tight for a long moment; then pulling away from her, he looked into her eyes and asked, "What about Juan?"

Dolores told him what had happened after he left, saying that she hated to hurt Juan, but her love for Tony was too strong. She had to be in his arms once again.

Tony whispered into her ear, "I am sorry for Juan, but I read in your eyes that you still loved me."

"I will always love you, Tony," she admitted.

They gazed at each other for a long moment before finally kissing—first tentatively, then passionately.

Hugging her tightly, Tony declared, "Ah, my life is happy once again. I am free, I have a new job—and I have you, my wonderful, beautiful Dolores."

Dolores kissed Tony one more time, then told him that she had to get back to her aunt. "We will meet again tomorrow, my love," she promised as she climbed onto her horse and rode home.

Tony stood gazing after Dolores, a smile of contentment on his lips. He had just turned toward the house and started for the porch, whistling happily, when Juan Gomez suddenly came galloping into the yard.

By the look on his face it was apparent that Juan was about to explode. Jumping down off his horse, the big Mexican stomped toward Tony. While shaking a threatening finger in Tony's face, he blared, "I was halfway home when I decided to turn around and come see you, Lucero. I want you to know that I think Dolores is being a foolish, impetuous woman! You are going to make her miserable because your kind never learn. You will be back behind bars again, and then she will be alone. I am telling you to get out of her life and let her marry a man who will not break her heart!"

Tony's own anger surfaced. Glaring at Juan, he growled, "You are neither my judge nor my jury, Gomez! I love Dolores more than life itself, and I am not going to break her heart! What is more, Dolores loves me, and you are not going to order me out of her life!"

Without warning, Juan attacked Tony. Balling his fists, he caught him on the jaw with a solid punch, and the smaller man went down onto his knees, shaking his head.

Carmen, who had been watching from the porch, screamed at the sight of her injured son. Manuel dashed out of the house to see what had caused his wife to scream, stopping short at the sight of the big man assaulting Tony. He shouted Juan's name, begging him to leave Tony alone, but the big Mexican's anger made him immune to Manuel's pleas.

Juan Gomez's size gave him a clear advantage over Tony. Holding him down by straddling him, he pummeled Tony with his fists. At the sight of her beloved son being brutalized, Carmen Lucero ran off the porch like a woman possessed, screaming Tony's name. Throwing all caution aside, she leapt on the big Mexican's back, clawing at his eyes. But Gomez elbowed her savagely and sent her tumbling behind him.

Tony's face was cut, bruised, and bleeding. When Juan Gomez started to batter him again, Manuel Lucero raced up behind the burly man and pulled Juan's revolver out of its holster, jamming it into his back. "That's enough, Gomez!" railed Manuel, poking the gun hard into the big Mexican. "Hit him one more time, and I'll kill you!"

Breathing hard, Juan released Tony and turned his head, glaring at the older man. He had a fist cocked, ready to deliver another blow to Tony, who was barely conscious. When the big Mexican looked as if he did not believe Manuel would shoot him, the angry father lined up the barrel of the revolver between his eyes and hissed, "I mean it, Gomez! I will shoot you if you don't get off my son right now." His eyes narrowing with fury, Manuel declared, "Furthermore, I'm taking you to the marshal's office to press charges. There are laws against coming onto a man's property and assaulting him or his family."

Juan Gomez hesitated only a moment, then rose to his feet. Gasping for air, he explained, "You have to understand, Mr. Lucero. Dolores and I were to be married in a few weeks. Now I have lost her. If Tony had not come home, she would have been my wife."

"That doesn't give you the right to beat my son to a pulp, Gomez!" retorted Manuel. "Start walking. You know where the marshal's office is. Head for it!"

Marshal Dan Washburn was seated at his desk when Manuel Lucero prodded Juan Gomez into the marshal's office with the revolver trained on his back.

Dan Washburn rose, rounded the desk, and demanded, "What's going on here?"

Quickly Manuel Lucero told the marshal what had happened.

Fixing Gomez with a hard glare, the lawman agreed, "Juan, Manuel is absolutely right. You have overstepped your bounds. No matter what has happened between you and Tony over Dolores, you had no right to attack him." Looking at the smaller man, he asked, "Are you going to press charges?"

Manuel was going to answer yes, but he had thought the matter over during the walk to town and changed his mind. Trying to put himself in Juan's place, he could understand how deeply the man was hurt by the sudden turn of events. Tony was at the core of it, so naturally he was Juan's target. Sighing, Manuel replied, "I do not know how badly my son is hurt, Marshal. It is not my wish to cause undue trouble for Juan, so if he will pay whatever doctor bills may come from this and apologize to my son, I will not press charges."

Washburn stared unwaveringly at Juan for a long moment, then said, "You heard him, Juan. How about it?"

Juan growled, "I will pay the doctor bills—but I will *not* apologize. There is nothing to apologize for!"

"Then you can think about your decision in a cell," Washburn snapped, taking the big Mexican's arm and guiding him toward the rear of the building.

Moments later the marshal returned to the office, shaking his head. "He's really hot, Manuel, so I think a few days in jail will help cool him off. Whew! He cussed me out good when I put him in the cell. Let me know how Tony is, won't you?"

"I will," replied Manuel, handing over the revolver. "Here. This is Juan's. I guess you can give it back to him when you release him." He headed for the door, then paused with his hand grasping the knob, half turning around. "Tony wants to talk with you," he informed the lawman. "He may try to see you when he comes to work for your brother on Monday morning . . . if he is able to work." He smiled sadly, adding, "Tony is a good boy, Marshal. I hope that one day soon everyone here in Raton will know that."

"I hope so, too, Manuel."

Chapter Six

After dinner that night, U.S. Marshal Ben Bryce and Lisa Washburn sat together in the swing on the front porch of the Washburn house under a sky dotted with myriad twinkling stars. As Bryce recounted some of his exciting experiences as a federal lawman, Lisa gazed at him with awe and admiration—and attraction. Her eye was caught by the figure of a man coming along the street, and as he came closer, she recognized Deputy Ned Mills. She stiffened, annoyed that Mills persisted in making a nuisance of himself, but nonetheless she would make an attempt to be civil to him.

"Hello," Mills said as he drew up to the porch. It was evident from the expression on his face that he was miffed to find Lisa sitting in the swing with Bryce, but he tried to cover it. Smiling warmly at Lisa, he told her, "I was hoping we could take a walk together on such a beautiful night."

The beautiful blonde did not want to go anywhere with Mills, but for courtesy's sake she agreed. With a reluctant sigh she stood, giving Bryce a small smile. As she stepped off the porch, her two brothers came through the front gate, and she and Mills greeted them. Dave and Bob explained that they had returned to the store to do some work after supper, then decided to stop by and see their parents on their way home to their respective houses.

"Ned and I will only be gone a short while," Lisa told them pointedly, "so perhaps you'll still be here when I get back." With that she swept through the gate with the deputy.

Mills offered Lisa his arm, but she did not take it. They were about a half block from the Washburn house when the deputy remarked rather stiffly, "I don't mind telling you, Lisa, I'll be glad when Ben Bryce leaves."

The young woman knew the reason, but she pretended otherwise, asking innocently, "Why? Do you have something against him?"

"As a matter of fact, I do," he replied tartly. "I don't like the way he looks at you, and I don't like him spending so much time with you."

Lisa felt her temper rising. Struggling to maintain her composure, she retorted, "What business is it of yours, Ned?"

Mills stopped short, a shocked expression on his face. Lisa kept on walking, and the deputy hurried to catch up to her. Taking hold of her arm, he pulled her to a halt. "Now just a minute!" he gasped. "What do you mean, what business is it of mine? What about our relationship? I mean, after all, you know that I love you!"

Jerking her arm free, Lisa snapped, "You may recall that I never said that those feelings were reciprocated. You, of course, may love whomever you wish—but that does *not* mean that the person you love necessarily returns that love."

Pouting, the deputy responded, "Well, you certainly have spent a lot of time in my company. We've taken many walks together, and I've eaten with your family . . . ."

Shaking her head, Lisa informed him, "I have been friendly to you, Ned, because I had no reason to be *unfriendly.* I see now that I made a mistake. That only encouraged you to assume more than you should have."

The deputy sniffed derisively. "You've done far more

than merely encourage me. What about all those kisses you've given me?"

Lisa started with surprise. "Kisses? You mean those little pecks on the cheek I've given you a few times? Really, Ned, I don't know how you could have assumed they meant anything beyond friendship. I've never said a word to indicate otherwise. In fact—"

"In fact what?"

The blonde hesitated for a moment, then sighed. "Well, I may as well be forthright. I've not wanted to say this to you before because I didn't want to hurt you, but my feelings toward you are those of a sister for her brother—nothing more."

They passed under a streetlamp, and Ned studied Lisa's face in the dim yellow light. Quietly he told her, "I know I could change how you feel toward me if you'd give me a chance."

Lisa chose not to respond to his statement—although she was thinking that even a dozen chances would not change her mind about Ned Mills. Turning around, she headed back toward her home. She glanced at the deputy, then suggested, "Maybe it would be best if we just didn't see each other at all, Ned. I have made no commitments to you, nor do I belong to you—and you're behaving quite to the contrary. Especially as regards Ben Bryce. Frankly, whom I choose to spend time with is simply none of your business."

"Okay, okay," he breathed. "I won't say anything anymore—as long as I can continue to see you."

"As a friend?"

"As a friend."

The young woman thought about it for a moment, then relented. "All right," she agreed reluctantly. "But if you overstep your bounds again, Ned, our friendship is finished."

They reached the Washburn house and turned into the walk, and Lisa smiled when she saw her father and brothers seated on the steps talking to Ben Bryce. She could tell by the expressions on their faces that they had been enjoying their talk, and she was pleased that her family seemed to like the young U.S. marshal as much as she did.

When Bryce saw Lisa, he stood up and asked, "Did you have a nice walk?"

Shrugging her shoulders, she replied offhandedly, "It was all right."

Dan Washburn flicked a glance at his deputy, and the light spilling from the porch light revealed a dismal and sour face. Getting to his feet, Raton's marshal declared, "Well, folks, it's my turn to make the rounds on Main Street. Guess I'd best get it done."

"I'll walk with you as far as my house," Ned Mills offered.

Lisa stepped onto the porch and yawned. She kissed her father's cheek, then announced, "Well, gentlemen, I'm going to bid you all good night." With that, she turned and went inside.

Leaving Bob and Dave Washburn with Ben Bryce, the two lawmen headed toward Main Street and soon faded into the night.

Marshal Dan Washburn said good night to his deputy at Mills's house, then proceeded to his office. Upon entering, he lit a lamp and went to check on his prisoner. Juan Gomez was stretched out on the cot in his cell, and at Washburn's entrance, the big Mexican stood up and walked to the bars.

The lawman spoke with Juan for a few minutes, and he decided that the jilted suitor had cooled down enough to release him. Before he unlocked the door, however, he asked, "Do I have your promise that you'll apologize to Tony Lucero?" Washburn looked him straight in the eye. "Do I have your word on that?"

"*Sí.* You have my word on it."

Nodding, Washburn announced, "All right, Juan.

You've never before gotten into any trouble, so I'm going to trust you."

After unlocking the cell door, Washburn led Juan Gomez to the office. Opening a drawer, he handed him his revolver and reiterated, "No more trouble between you and Tony, right?"

"I'll do my part," Juan assured him, slipping the gun into its holster. He nodded perfunctorily, then left.

After extinguishing the lamp, Dan Washburn stepped outside, locked the office door, and began his rounds. Raton's main street was dimly lit by kerosene lanterns hanging on poles along both sides of the street some seventy feet apart. Since the lampposts were at the edges of the boardwalks, more light was cast into the street than on the boardwalks themselves, but the lamps shed enough light to enable Dan to check the shops. The lawman had gone only a half block when he encountered six men coming out of Jack Fagan's gun and saddle shop, where they had been playing poker all evening. Standing with Fagan under a streetlamp were Abe Washburn, ranchers Cal Manley and Arthur Wellman, Weston DeRose, and Charlie Smith, who was Raton's pharmacist.

"Good evening, gentlemen," Dan greeted them cheerfully. "Who was the lucky winner tonight?"

Weston DeRose chuckled and replied, "Your brother."

Charlie Smith laughed and chided, "We all know Abe cheated, Dan, but he's so dad-blamed big, we're afraid to call his hand on it."

The rest of the men joined in the laughter.

"Well, fellas," Jack Fagan spoke up, "I've got to go home with my tail between my legs and confess to the little woman that I sent Abe home with every dollar I made in the shop today. Good night."

Abe laughed and called after him, "Tell Lucille that next time *she* can sit in on the game. I'd be afraid to cheat *her*."

Fagan's laughter trailed behind him as he walked away. Cal Manley and Abe Washburn chorused good night to the others, and then Manley untied his horse and mounted up and left while Abe headed up the street.

Dan Washburn chatted with Weston DeRose and Arthur Wellman for a few more moments, then he, too, moved on, checking doors along the boardwalk. He had gone only a short distance when a man emerged from the cross street just ahead and came toward him. He could not make out the man's identity until he stepped under a streetlamp, and then the lawman saw that it was Tony Lucero. The young man's face reflected the beating he had sustained earlier, for it was badly swollen, and there were cuts on his lips and cheekbones. He noted that Tony was wearing a sidearm, but he thought nothing of it. There was no law in New Mexico that a paroled man could not wear a gun, and nearly every man in and around Raton did so.

The lawman stepped off the boardwalk and met Tony in the middle of the street, where they stood in a circle of yellow light. "Hello, Tony," Dan said. "What are you doing here in town at this hour?"

"Hello, Marshal," Tony responded amiably, trying to smile although it was clearly painful for him to do so. "I wanted to see you, sir," the Mexican then explained. "I went by the house, and your sons told me you were making your rounds. I felt I would not be able to sleep tonight unless I squared things with you." He paused then asked, "Incidentally, is Juan still in jail?"

"No. I let him out when he promised he'd apologize to you."

Tony nodded. "Thank you. But to get back to what I was saying, five years ago I made a very rash statement about getting even with you for sending me to prison. I want to reaffirm that I spoke in the heat of passion, and I did not mean those things. I assure you that I have learned my lesson. I do not ever want to see the inside of a prison again, and I will never do anything that would endanger my freedom—and my life with Dolores."

"I'm glad to hear it, son," the marshal declared.

Tony continued, "Your brother has been very kind to give me a job, Marshal, and I am eager to work for him. It is my desire to make my family, Dolores, and the whole town proud of me."

"That's most admirable," agreed Dan. "But I must tell you that I'm worried about Juan. I think you ought to be wary of him—since we now know he has a pretty violent temper. Although he's trying not to show it, he's still angry about Dolores's going back to you."

"Thank you for your concern, Marshal. I will heed your warning."

Dan laid a hand on Tony's shoulder. "I want you to know that I think it most admirable that you came to see me tonight, Tony. You go on home now. And good luck at the blacksmith shop."

"Gracias," Tony responded. "Good night, Marshal."

"Good night," echoed Dan, turning his back to Tony to step onto the boardwalk.

Suddenly, from between two buildings, a shot was fired, shattering the stillness of the night. It was immediately followed by another. The slugs whizzed past Tony Lucero's head and slammed into Dan Washburn's back.

Seeing the marshal fall, Tony's first reaction was to draw the gun on his hip. Sure that he was the intended target, he braced himself, gun in hand, expecting more shots to follow from the unknown and unseen assailant. Instead, he heard Weston DeRose shout from down the block, "You! Stop!"

Tony whipped around, and he saw DeRose and Arthur Wellman racing toward him, pulling their weapons as they ran. Realizing that he was standing there holding his gun in his hand, making it appear as if he had just shot down the marshal, the young Mexican panicked.

He turned and darted into the dark shadows between the buildings on the side street and was quickly swallowed up by the night.

Wellman and DeRose dashed to the marshal, who was lying facedown in the street. They turned Dan Washburn over, and one look at his face told them the terrible story: He was dead.

Gesturing with his chin in the direction young Lucero had taken, Wellman growled, "No way to catch him in the dark, but we both saw who it was. His face was mighty clear under this streetlamp. He won't get away from us."

People began coming to the scene from every direction. At the sight of the fallen lawman the onlookers gasped, and several people asked if anyone had gone for the doctor. Turning to face the crowd, Weston DeRose told them grimly, "No reason to. The marshal's dead."

A collective cry rose from the crowd, and many people mindlessly echoed the word "dead."

Deputy Ned Mills came on the run, gun drawn and ready. Elbowing his way through the press of people, he demanded, "What's going on?" At the sight of the lifeless form of Dan Washburn, he swore and knelt beside him. Mills swore again, then stood up and looked around at the crowd. "Did anyone see what happened?"

"Arthur and I did," Weston DeRose told him.

Before Mills could continue with his questions, someone remarked, "Here come Dan's sons."

Bob Washburn arrived first, and the crowd parted to let him through. "Oh, my God!" he said hoarsely, seeing the corpse. Kneeling down beside his slain father, he murmured, "We heard the shots from Dad's house, and we knew he was doing his rounds so we came to see what happened." He swallowed hard, then added in a stunned voice, "I can't believe it. I just can't believe it."

Dave reached the scene just after his brother, in tandem with U.S. Marshal Ben Bryce.

"Dad!" exclaimed Dave, kneeling beside his older brother.

The brothers stared transfixed at the body for a long moment, incapable of speech. Then Bob looked up and managed to choke out, "Who did this?"

Nodding toward Arthur Wellman, Weston DeRose replied, "Art and I both saw who did it, Bob. It was Tony Lucero."

"Tony Lucero!" shouted Bob, standing up.

Lucero's name buzzed through the crowd.

Dave Washburn rose slowly, his face a mixture of grief and fury. Looking at DeRose, he told him, "That dirty, lying scum came by the house a short while ago. Said he wanted to see Dad and that he couldn't sleep until he'd squared things with him."

"He squared things, all right," grunted Bob. "Two bullets in the back."

Shaking his head, Dave said to DeRose, "He seemed so sincere. I never dreamed he would do this." His voice breaking, he added, "We should've come with him. We were wrong to let him see Dad alone."

Putting a steady hand on his brother's shoulder, Bob insisted, "We can't blame ourselves, Dave. Tony sure convinced me he wanted to make things right with Dad. How could we have known otherwise?"

Ben Bryce then looked at Wellman and DeRose and asked, "Are you gentlemen absolutely positive it was this Lucero fellow who shot the marshal?"

"No doubt about it," DeRose replied firmly. "Art and I were standing right over there in front of the gun shop, talking. We immediately turned at the sound of the shots, and standing over Dan, with a gun in his hand, was Tony Lucero. Saw him clear as day. And when we hollered, he ran."

Suddenly bowling his way through the crowd was Abe Washburn, but the giant of a man stopped in his tracks when he saw the body of the marshal. "Dan!" he screamed. "No!" He sank to his knees and cradled his brother's lifeless body in his arms. Holding Dan's head against his massive chest, the blacksmith moaned, "This isn't fair. Not Dan. He was such a good man." After a few minutes he gently laid the body back down, then got to his feet. His expression hardened, and swearing vociferously, he looked around at the people gathered, then focused on Ned Mills and blurted, "Who did it?"

"Tony Lucero," the deputy replied coldly. He then related Weston DeRose's story.

Abe growled, "So the little rat meant his threat against Dan after all. And to think I offered him a job. I was really convinced he wanted to walk straight and make something of his life." The huge man clenched his fists, then rasped, "I'm going after him. I'll bring his battered, bloody body back for all of you to see what happens to the man who murdered my brother!"

Ned Mills grabbed hold of Abe's arm. "Don't do it, Abe!" he warned. "Tony must be arrested and prosecuted by due process of the law."

The crowd, which had swelled in size, angrily protested. Several people agreed that Abe should go after young Lucero and exact his revenge. One man shouted, "I say let Abe beat him up good, then we lynch him on the hangin' tree!"

Weston DeRose raised his hands and shouted above the clamor, "Wait a minute! Do I have to remind all of you of Leo Dunn's sickening death? There'll be no more hangings on that tree!"

Herman Franks, the bank president, had joined the throng, and he stepped beside DeRose, joining forces with him, and proclaimed, "You people are talking about vigilante justice! Dan Washburn would be furious if he could hear what you're proposing! He would never want you to bypass the law and lynch a man . . . even his own killer!"

A loud voice retaliated, "Tony deserves to be lynched! He shot down the marshal in cold blood . . . and in the back!"

There was a roar of agreement from the crowd. Deputy Ned Mills broke into a cold sweat, and it was clear that he was fearing the crowd would turn into an uncontrollable lynch mob.

Suddenly U.S. Marshal Ben Bryce shouted above the din, "Hold on, everybody! Let me remind you would-be executioners that I am a federal marshal! If there is a lynching party, every man in it will be arrested for murder—and then *you'll* hang!"

Bryce's sharp warning had an immediate effect, and the people cooled down quickly.

Still burning with hatred, Abe Washburn fumed, "Marshal Bryce, somebody has to go after Tony and catch him, so I'll do it. I won't kill him, but he might have an 'accident' on the way back and get banged up some."

Dave Washburn shook his head. "Uncle Abe, that would still be wrong. We need to let the law handle this. You know that's the way Dad would want it."

Abe's face was stony. "But Dave—"

"No buts, Uncle Abe," insisted Dave. "The man lying there in the dirt is my father, and believe me, I want his killer brought to justice as much as you do. But there's a right way to do it—and that's by the letter of the law."

The federal man put his hand on the blacksmith's arm. "Look, Abe, it's only human to want revenge over the cold-blooded murder of your brother—and to want to exact that revenge yourself. But Tony Lucero must stand trial." Turning to Ned Mills, he asked, "Have you any idea where Lucero might be?"

"He'll probably head for his father's house first, then no doubt he'll run for the mountains."

Herman Franks declared, "What are you waiting for, Ned? It's your job to catch him, and you'd best do it."

Ned Mills looked around. Every eye in the crowd was focused on him. Clearing his throat, he admitted, "Well, as you all know, I don't have that much experience as a lawman . . . nor in tracking lawbreakers down." He then looked at Ben Bryce, and it was clear that he was trying to hide his dislike for the man. "Marshal, would you ride with me to the Lucero place?"

"I'll be glad to," responded Bryce. "If we have to give chase, I may have a problem with these stitches pulling at my wound, but I'll help you all I can."

The banker suggested, "Marshal Bryce, maybe we'd better form a posse immediately."

"That won't be necessary at the moment," advised Bryce. "If Ned and I don't find Tony at the Lucero home, he'll already be on the run for the mountains, and there'd be nothing we could do till morning anyway. Let's just hope we can catch him at his father's place."

"I'm going with you and Ned to Manuel's," demanded Abe Washburn.

"No, you wait here with the others," countered Bryce, authority in his voice. "We'll be back shortly . . . with or without Tony Lucero."

As the two lawmen walked away to get their horses, Bob Washburn turned to his uncle. His eyes were still filled with stunned disbelief as he asked, "Will you go find Wilbur Nicely and ask him if he would come for Dad? Dave and I need to go break the awful news to Mom and the rest of the family."

"Sure thing, Bob," Abe replied, putting a consoling hand on his nephew's shoulder.

The two young men then hurried away, and the blacksmith stood watching them for a long moment. His face was grim as he finally sighed and headed toward the undertaking parlor. He had gone only a few steps when he stopped and turned back to the remaining crowd. "Folks!" he called, and everyone looked his way. "I just realized something. Lucero might not have gone home. He's sweet on that Domingo girl, so maybe he's gone to her house. After all, it's just a few blocks away."

"That's a mighty smart thought, Abe," spoke up Harold Bentley.

The burly man looked at his fellow townsmen and asked, "How many of you have your guns on you?"

When a number of men responded, Abe suggested, "Okay, then. Let's go see if we can find my brother's killer."

Weston DeRose stepped in front of the big man and cautioned, "Abe, I don't think you should do this. Going after Tony is a job for the law."

"The law's heading for the Lucero place," argued Abe. "If I'm right, Bryce and Mills are on a wild-goose chase—and Tony could run for the mountains from the Domingo house and maybe get away with murder."

"But you have no authority to go after Tony," protested DeRose.

"No authority?" roared Abe. "He killed my brother, didn't he?" Then, calming slightly, he added, "Don't worry. We'll capture him alive—if possible. We won't shoot unless he shoots first."

Gesturing for the others to follow him, Abe Washburn began walking swiftly toward Flora Domingo's house. By the light of the moon that had just risen in the clear sky, the twelve well-armed men wended their way through the silent streets of Raton.

No one noticed Juan Gomez standing in the deep shadows between two buildings, listening. Gloating within, the husky Mexican told himself he would soon be rid of Tony Lucero . . . and Dolores Domingo would once again be his.

Chapter Seven

Dolores Domingo sat reading in the parlor while her aunt slept soundly in the next room. Although it was getting late, the young woman's thoughts and emotions were swirling, and sleep was eluding her. Her thoughts were suddenly interrupted by the muffled sound of two gunshots from the direction of Main Street. She closed her book and listened, but there were no other shots. A few minutes passed, and then—although the words were indistinct—she heard the sound of many excited voices.

Suddenly there was an insistent knock at the door. Putting down her book, Dolores hurried to answer the summons, whispering loudly, "Who is it?"

"Tony!" came the anxious reply. "Please let me in!"

Dolores slid the bolt and opened the door, gasping at the sight of Tony's bruised face. He darted in, gasping for breath and ordering, "Close the door! Quick! And douse the lamp!"

As Dolores ran across the room to extinguish the lamp, Flora Domingo came into the parlor, rubbing her eyes. "What is it?" she asked, her voice thick with sleep. "I heard someone knocking. Who was— Tony! What are you doing here? Your face! What happened to you?"

"I was about to ask the same thing," Dolores remarked as she doused the lamp. Waiting a moment for her eyes to adjust to the dark, she walked back across the room to Tony and gripped his hands. "What has happened?" she asked.

Trembling, young Lucero told them what had occurred, starting with Juan Gomez's coming to his house and attacking him and ending with Dan Washburn's murder. He emphasized that the two bullets that hit the marshal had come from behind him, barely missing him.

"The men who called out for you to stop, did they recognize you?" asked Dolores.

"Probably, since we were standing under the streetlamp. Although it all happened so fast that I'm not completely sure."

She thought for a moment, then her hand went to her mouth. "Perhaps *you* were the target, Tony! After all, you said the bullets barely missed you."

Shaking his head, the young man replied, "At first I thought that as well. I thought that Gomez was not finished with me after all. But then I realized that whoever it was who shot Marshal Washburn had plenty of opportunity to fire at me as well—if he had shot the marshal by mistake." He lovingly touched Dolores's face, then told her, "I've got to run away from Raton and never return. I came to ask you to go with me."

Dolores was horrified. "Tony," she breathed, "I love you enough to run away with you, but if you run now, you will have to run for the rest of your life."

"But, Dolores—"

Flora stepped beside Tony and put her hand on his shoulder. "Listen to her!" she pleaded. "If you are innocent, you must not run. You must face the townspeople and tell them what happened."

"But they will not believe me!" Tony replied, his voice shaking. "The reception many of them gave me when I arrived in town today proves that they are already against me. They will not be convinced that the threat I made to Marshal Washburn five years ago has long been forgotten."

"Tony, perhaps he is not dead," Flora suggested. "If this is so, you have nothing to fear."

Looking thoughtful, Tony replied, "I suppose it is possible that he is alive—but what if he is not?"

Tears welled up in Dolores's eyes. "Tony, surely somehow you can prove your innocence!"

Peering at her face illuminated by the moonlight streaming through the window, Tony muttered, "I don't know how I can do that—which is why I must leave."

Flora advised, "As you said, perhaps the marshal is alive. If he is not, somehow we will find a way to prove you did not do it. But if you do not immediately go and turn yourself in to Deputy Mills—if you run—you will only look guilty."

Tony stared out the window for a moment. Turning, he looked first at Dolores, then her aunt. Sighing, he agreed, "All right, I will do it."

Dolores put her hand on Tony's arm. "I have just thought of something. Perhaps someone in this town wanted the marshal dead—and he knew of your threat, making it look as though you are guilty."

"That may be so," agreed Tony. "But it is more likely that whoever shot the marshal was out to frame me and see me go back to prison. Maybe Marshal Washburn just had to pay the price for that to happen."

Flora interjected, "That does not make sense, Tony. If the man who shot Marshal Washburn was simply trying to get rid of you, would he not have just shot you instead of the marshal?"

Shaking his head, Tony sighed, "That is probably true. This is all too much for me, and I cannot think clearly. I will go now and turn myself in to the deputy. One thing is for sure: Whoever did the shooting must be caught—and the sooner it is obvious that I am innocent, the sooner the real criminal will be arrested."

"I will go with you," volunteered Dolores.

"Maybe it is best that you stay here," Flora quickly put in.

"I must go, Aunt Flora," insisted Dolores, moving toward the door beside Tony. "I want to be with him when he tells the story to Deputy Mills."

"All right, dear. But come back as soon as you can and let me know what has happened." Flora Domingo stood on her tiptoes and kissed Tony Lucero on the cheek. "Go with God," she murmured.

The young couple held hands as they left the house and headed toward Main Street. They had walked nearly a block when, by the moonlight, they saw Abe Washburn and his followers coming toward them. Abe and his group obviously spotted the couple at the same time, for they stopped short and raised their guns.

"Halt!" Abe bellowed. "Hold it right there, Lucero!"

Tony tensed up, but Dolores reassured him, "Don't worry, they'll believe you."

The young Mexican nodded and waited.

The group of men walked slowly toward them, and Abe called, "Now reach down real slow and unbuckle your gun belt, Lucero, and let it fall." He paused, then added, "Dolores, step away from him."

"Please, Mr. Washburn," Dolores whimpered. "Tony did not shoot your brother. We were heading to the marshal's office, and he was going to turn himself in to Deputy Mills. Is the deputy with you?"

Harold Bentley suddenly elbowed his way in front of the others and shouted sharply, "He's lying if he said he didn't shoot Dan Washburn, Dolores! There were two eyewitnesses who saw Tony shoot the marshal in the back."

"Like I said, Lucero," the blacksmith broke in, "drop your gun belt." When Tony hesitated, Abe roared, "Now!"

Dolores let go of Tony's hand and took a step forward. "We want to see Deputy Mills!"

"He's not here," growled Abe. "He went out to the

Lucero house, looking for your murdering boyfriend. And I'd advise you to get away from Tony, Dolores."

"Tony is not a murderer, Mr. Washburn!" Dolores retorted. "You are wrong! When the shots were fired, he got scared and ran because he was sure everyone would think he had done it—and it looks as though he was right!"

Realizing that he still did not know for certain what Dan Washburn's condition was, Tony asked, "Is Marshal Washburn dead?"

The feisty Bentley spat, "Sure he's dead, you bloody killer! You put two slugs in his back! Now get that gun belt off like Abe told you, or we'll shoot you down where you stand!"

Sweat broke out on Tony Lucero's forehead. Purposely holding his hand away from his holster, he insisted, "I am innocent, Mr. Washburn! I want to turn myself in to the law, and I am not dropping my gun belt and I am not moving from this spot until you bring Deputy Mills!"

Weston DeRose spoke up. "Listen to the kid, Abe. Wait until Ned Mills gets here and don't do anything. Tony's scared, so take it easy."

Abe snarled, "What do you mean, take it easy? Did *he* take it easy with my brother?" Glaring at Tony, the blacksmith declared, "Our bringing Mills won't change a thing, Lucero! You killed Dan just like you threatened to do five years ago . . . and you're gonna hang!" Most of the men with the blacksmith began cheering him on.

Raising his gun, Harold Bentley snarled, "I'd advise you to drop your weapon, Lucero, 'cause if you don't, this here one's gonna get you good!"

Panic was quickly rising in young Lucero, for he knew he did not have a chance. The whole town would believe he was guilty, and they would hang him for sure. Afraid for his life, he whispered to Dolores, "Forgive me, my dearest. I have no choice but to flee."

"No, Tony!" she whispered urgently. "Don't do it! They will shoot you down!"

Shaking his head, he countered, "It is my only chance. Once they get their hands on me, I am a doomed man." He then added in a trembling voice, "I love you!" With that he pivoted and ran.

The angry townsmen brought their guns to bear, and Abe Washburn shouted, "Stop right there, Lucero!" But the young Mexican kept on running, and the blacksmith roared, "Get him, men!"

Just as they were about to open fire, Dolores darted after Tony, pleading with him to come back. At the same instant, Weston DeRose shouted, "Don't shoot, men! You'll hit the girl!" But his words came too late. Several of the men, their fingers pressing their triggers, fired reflexively, and their guns roared. Dolores Domingo stopped short and screamed, her back arching, then crumpled to the ground.

"You stupid fools!" DeRose bellowed. "You got Dolores!"

Hearing the young woman's scream, Tony froze in his tracks and whipped around. At the sight of Dolores's fallen body, he shrieked her name and ran toward her, crying out, "Don't shoot! Don't shoot! You could hit her again!"

But two of the men ignored him and raised their weapons, and a bullet hummed past Tony's head like an angry hornet. Skidding to a halt, he whipped out his own gun and railing at them, shot back at the men. He got off four slugs, then turned around and began running in the other direction. He dashed through a yard and over a fence, disappearing from sight.

Running up the residential street, Tony Lucero found a saddled horse tied in front of a house, and he quickly untied the reins and leapt onto the animal's back. He gouged the horse's sides with his bootheels and put it into a gallop, heading east out of town. With tears running down his face as he rode, he wondered over and over if Dolores was dead or alive. And if she was still alive, how badly was she injured? One thing he was sure of: He would never see his beloved again.

Two of Tony Lucero's bullets had found their marks when he fired at the band of pursuers. Lloyd Landers, a teller at the Raton Community Bank, and Clarence Moon, day clerk at the Raton Hotel, were both down. Seeing that several of the other men were tending them, Abe Washburn quickly ran to where Dolores Domingo lay.

He bent over Dolores and saw that she was still breathing. "How bad is it, girl?" he asked gently.

Dolores was conscious, but in shock, and she could not answer.

Weston DeRose came up beside Abe and snapped, "You should've listened to me! You should have left it to the lawmen, not aroused a bunch of addlepated citizens to go off half-cocked!" He shook his head angrily, adding, "You said there wouldn't be any shooting unless Tony fired first. Well, Tony *didn't* fire the first shot, and your hot head has put three people down with bullets in them!"

"It wasn't *my* hot head that caused this!" snarled the huge man. "It was Harold Bentley's hot head!"

"Bentley's the one that got Landers and Moon shot, Abe," growled DeRose, "but it was the whole bunch of you who are responsible for this poor girl's getting hit! If you hadn't come storming after Tony but had let the law handle it, she wouldn't be lying here right now with lead in her back!"

"Aw, shut up!" barked Abe. He turned around and called to the cluster of men, "How are those two?"

"Lloyd isn't too bad, Abe," one of the men replied. "He was just hit in the shoulder. But Clarence wasn't so lucky. Tim's gone for Doc Townsend."

"Good thinking," responded the blacksmith. He stood up and told Weston DeRose, "You stay with the girl." Then he faced the others, instructing, "A couple of you men wait with Lloyd and Clarence for Doc. The rest of you come with me. We're going after Tony."

From a block away came the sudden sound of galloping hooves, and Abe Washburn cursed loudly. Ordering the men to follow him, he dashed up the street and through the yard where Tony Lucero had gone. There he found a man standing outside his house, his fist raised in anger, swearing.

Rushing up to the man, Abe demanded, "Was that Tony Lucero we just heard riding away?"

The man turned and glared at the blacksmith. "How should *I* know? It was too dark to see. All I *do* know is someone stole my horse and took off on him." Shaking his fist, he snarled, "Where's the marshal? I want him going after that thief right now, and I don't care how late it is!"

"The marshal's dead," muttered Abe.

"Dead?" echoed the man, his mouth dropping open in disbelief.

"Yeah," replied the blacksmith, "and it was Tony Lucero who killed him. Put two bullets in his back. A bunch of us were pursuing him, but then a couple of my men were shot by Lucero."

"Well, somebody's got to go after him!" exclaimed the man. "Where's Ned Mills?"

"He rode out to Manuel's place, thinking the kid would probably hightail it there before he headed for parts unknown. Once he finds he's been giving chase in the wrong direction, he'll be back."

Throwing up his hands, Abe declared to the men, "I guess we better get back to the others. No sense standing here watching the dust settle. We'll wait for Mills and Bryce to return and meet with them to discuss forming a posse in the morning."

Bentley shook his head. "I don't know, Abe. Ned's a good kid, but he's not had any experience in leading a posse."

"Yeah, I've been thinking about that. Maybe we can convince Bryce to head it—after all, he is the territorial marshal for these parts."

Returning to the others, the men found that the physician had arrived—as had Flora Domingo. She had heard the shots and, fearing the worst, had gone to see what had happened. The Mexican woman was standing over her niece, wringing her hands and weeping, while Dolores, now wrapped in a blanket, was lying still, her eyes closed.

A number of other townspeople, some holding lanterns, had come on the scene and were silently clustered around the victims. Dr. John Townsend was tending the unconscious Clarence Moon, while Lloyd Landers, who had a temporary bandage on his right shoulder, sat watching.

Finally the doctor stood up and looked around at the crowd. "All right. Let's get them to my office so I can begin surgery."

Flora Domingo followed as two men carried the stretcher bearing her niece. The wives of Lloyd Landers and Clarence Moon had been summoned, and they arrived just as some men began bearing their husbands to Townsend's office. The physician reassured Jane Landers that her husband, who had a slug in his right shoulder, was not in danger. When Edie Moon asked about her husband, Townsend replied evasively, "Let's get him back to my office. I'll be better able to assess Clarence's condition there."

When Edie hurried to walk beside her husband, Abe Washburn and Weston DeRose flanked the physician. DeRose asked, "What do you really think about Clarence? Will he make it?"

Lowering his voice so it would not carry to Edie, Townsend replied, "I don't think so. I could be wrong, but I have a feeling that bullet has torn him up something fierce inside."

"How about Dolores?" queried Abe.

The doctor shook his head sadly. "Bad," he replied glumly, "real bad."

"Is she gonna die, Doc?"

"She'll live, but that pretty little gal will never walk again."

DeRose gasped, "Oh, my God! Are you sure?"

Townsend sighed. "Unfortunately, yes. The bullet caught her from the side and severed her spinal cord. She's permanently paralyzed from the waist down."

Abe Washburn swore under his breath, then said, "Poor kid. Could she be helped if we could get her back east to one of those fancy surgeons, Doc?"

"No, Abe," came Townsend's flat answer. "When the spinal cord has been severed as Dolores's is, there's nothing anyone can do. She simply will never walk again." He paused, then added, "Of course, it could have been worse. If she hadn't caught the bullet from the side, it would have ripped into her and no doubt would have killed her."

Weston DeRose mused, "I guess when I shouted, she must have turned slightly. Otherwise, the slug would have caught her square."

"Dumb numskulls shouldn't have been shooting with that girl in the line of fire," the physician said acidly.

Abe and DeRose exchanged glances. The land developer's eyes clearly placed the blame on the blacksmith's shoulders. Dropping away from Townsend as the procession reached his office, the two men stood looking at each other.

Uncomfortable under DeRose's harsh gaze, Abe announced, "Look, Wes, Tony Lucero's responsible for this, not me. If he hadn't shot my brother in the back, none of the rest of this would have happened."

"You're satisfied that you were right to lead those men after Tony even though not a one of you wore a badge?"

Abe hesitated for a moment, then said defensively,

"With both lawmen out of town, I figured I had to act on my instinct that Lucero'd be at Dolores's. I was sure right about that, wasn't I?"

"Were you and the others right to cut loose with your guns when Dolores was in the line of fire?" asked DeRose crustily.

Abe's eyes narrowed angrily. "It was an accident. We were doing our duty, trying to stop that cold-blooded killer from getting away."

DeRose shrugged. Walking toward the doctor's office, he muttered, "I sure hope you'll be able to sleep nights."

Abe Washburn stood watching his friend's retreating back for a few moments. Then, jamming his hands into his pockets, he, too, headed for John Townsend's clinic.

Chapter Eight

U.S. Marshal Ben Bryce and Deputy Ned Mills quickly covered the short distance to the Lucero house, and dismounting, they hurried to the front door and knocked loudly. Manuel opened the door, and the smile on his face immediately faded, replaced by a look of concern at the sight of the two lawmen.

"Is Tony here, Mr. Lucero?" Mills asked, ignoring ceremony.

"No, he isn't," replied Manuel. "He walked to town a while ago, to speak to Marshal Washburn."

The two lawmen eyed each other, then the federal man said, "Mr. Lucero, I am United States Marshal Ben Bryce. If your son is hiding here, or if he has returned to gather some possessions and then make his escape, you will be in deep trouble if you cover for him."

Manuel suddenly looked very frightened. "Marshal, what has happened? Has Tony done something wrong?"

Ned Mills stared at the small man, then demanded, "Mr. Lucero, if Tony came back here, you must tell us. We—"

"We have not seen Tony since he left about an hour ago, Deputy," Carmen Lucero interrupted, stepping beside her husband.

"What has happened?" Manuel asked again.

Bryce pushed back his hat and answered, "There's been a shooting. Marshal Washburn is dead."

Manuel gasped, then queried, "What has that got to do with Tony?"

"Witnesses saw your son talking to the marshal on the street, Mr. Lucero," replied Bryce. "Two shots were fired—and Tony was standing over the marshal's body with his gun in his hand."

Carmen Lucero clutched the crucifix that hung on a chain around her neck and crossed herself, murmuring something indecipherable in Spanish.

"It is not true!" Manuel shouted. "My boy would not shoot the marshal! Tony would not do this thing!"

"He tried to kill a man with a knife five years ago, didn't he?" rasped Mills.

"He was drunk then," Manuel countered in his son's defense. "He was not drinking tonight. I tell you, he did not shoot the marshal!"

"Then why did he run away?" asked the deputy.

"I do not know," confessed Manuel, shaking his head. "We must find him!"

"Don't worry, sir, we will," Bryce advised.

The two men turned to leave, and Mills instructed, "If he should show up here, you must talk him into turning himself in. It will only go worse for him if he runs."

"Maybe by now Tony is waiting at your office to turn himself in," Manuel suggested. "Maybe . . . maybe he ran because he was afraid, but he thought it over and went back. I will go with you."

Carmen Lucero began to weep. Taking his wife into his arms, Manuel tried to reassure her that everything would be all right. "I will be back as soon as I can," he promised. Then he followed the lawmen out of the house.

Quickly saddling his horse, Manuel rode into town with Bryce and Mills. As they headed along Main Street, they saw the large group gathered by Dr. John Townsend's office and slowed their horses to a walk. Abe Washburn spotted them and called them over, filling the lawmen in on what had happened while they were gone.

Manuel murmured, "I cannot believe this. My heart is heavy for poor Dolores. This terrible tragedy has befallen her because she loyally stayed by Tony's side."

The blacksmith said to Ben Bryce, "We'll need to mount a posse to go after Lucero, Marshal, and Ned will be the first to admit he hasn't had much experience with this sort of thing. Will you lead the men?"

"All right," agreed Bryce. "Get as many volunteers as you can, and tell them we'll head out at dawn. But keep in mind that if my wound opens up, I'll have to turn back and leave Ned in charge."

Manuel turned to Bryce and declared, "Marshal, I fear for my son's life. These men have hatred in their eyes, and I am afraid they will go after Tony to kill him, not to bring him in for trial."

Harold Bentley heard him and ventured sharply, "We'll probably *have* to kill him. After all, we gave him a chance to drop his gun belt before and he didn't, so it's not too likely he'll react any different when we catch up to him."

Weston DeRose turned to Bentley and lashed back, "Tony hadn't fired at us until you cut loose, you hot-headed fool! You might even say it's your fault that Lloyd and Clarence are lying in Doc's place with bullets in them right now and Dolores Domingo is crippled for life!"

"*My* fault?" roared Bentley. "I didn't shoot Lloyd and Clarence, Tony did! *After* the craven coward shot the marshal in the back!"

Manuel Lucero exploded, "Tony did not kill the marshal!"

Snorting derisively, Bentley railed back, "That kid of yours obviously has pulled the wool over your eyes,

Lucero. Otherwise you wouldn't be so blind to the fact that he's a killer!"

Without warning, Manuel lashed out with his fist, catching Harold Bentley on the jaw and sending him reeling back into the circle of men. Swearing vehemently, Bentley scrambled to his feet, his eyes blazing.

Ben Bryce urged Ned Mills, "You'd better stop this before somebody gets hurt."

Mills hesitated, and it was clear from the look in his eyes that he was afraid. In the meantime, Harold Bentley charged at the smaller Mexican and punched him on the nose. Manuel backtracked from the blow, then came again with both fists pumping. The two men traded punches for a few moments, then the bigger man got in a solid blow to Manuel's jaw, and he went down.

The men who stood around looked to Ned Mills to step in, as did Ben Bryce. When the deputy continued to hesitate, the federal man disregarded the wound in his side and stepped in. He blocked Harold Bentley's path as he headed for Manuel to hit him again as the Mexican was getting up.

Bentley was blind with rage. "Get outta my way!" he screamed at Bryce, and stomped toward him as if to bowl him over.

Ben Bryce had been in more fights than Harold Bentley would ever see—and he was all muscle and most of his strength had returned since being shot. Bracing himself, he sent a rocking punch to Bentley's jaw. Men in the group winced as bone met flesh with a sickening crack. Harold Bentley dropped to the ground, stunned.

Bryce straightened himself, running a hand along his wounded side as if testing it. When Weston DeRose asked if he had hurt himself, the marshal grinned crookedly and answered, "A little, but I'll be all right."

One of the men standing over Bentley whistled softly and announced to the others, "Remind me to stay on the marshal's good side, will you, boys?"

His remark was met with a rumble of appreciative laughter.

Manuel Lucero was on his feet, rubbing his jaw. Confronting Bryce, he insisted, "Marshal, you must not let Harold Bentley or any other man who is dead set on killing my boy ride in the posse. I know Tony did not kill Marshal Washburn. He must have a chance for a trial."

Abe Washburn spat in the dust and rasped, "Harold's right, Manuel! Your son's got you blinded. He killed my brother, all right!"

"No!" retorted Manuel. "Tony came into town eager to make things right with the marshal."

The blacksmith shook his head. "The only thing he was eager to do was make good his threat!"

Manuel Lucero's eyes filled with tears as his shoulders slumped in defeat. Ben Bryce laid a hand on his arm and promised, "Like I told you, Mr. Lucero, I'll be riding with the posse. I'll do everything in my power to bring your son back safely and see that he gets a fair trial."

One of the men said loudly, "A trial would be a waste of time, Marshal. Art Wellman and Wes DeRose are upstanding and respected in this community, and if they say they saw Tony Lucero shoot the marshal, then Lucero shot the marshal."

"No!" blurted Manuel. "They are mistaken! My boy is not a murderer!"

Abe Washburn's deep voice countered, "He went to prison for attempted murder, Manuel! And Clarence Moon is hanging between life and death. If he dies, your son will have two murders to pay for!"

"That won't hold up," U.S. Marshal Ben Bryce interjected. "From the way I heard it, Tony was firing in self-defense when he hit those two men. Didn't you tell me, Mr. DeRose, that Tony was shouting for them not to shoot when he was running back toward Dolores?"

"That's right," DeRose replied, nodding. "But Harold

—and then a couple of others—fired at Tony, causing him to shoot back."

"Let's keep it all in perspective, though, Marshal," countered Abe Washburn. "I ordered Lucero to drop his gun belt, but he didn't. If he had, none of these other shootings would have taken place—so the way I see it, he's as guilty as sin."

"Something keeps bothering me about this whole thing," murmured Bryce. Turning to Weston DeRose, he asked, "Exactly where were you and Mr. Wellman standing when you saw the shooting?"

Pointing with a forefinger, DeRose replied, "Right in front of Fagan's gun shop."

The marshal studied the spot closely, then asked, "Right under that streetlamp?"

"Yes."

"And you and Mr. Wellman recognized Tony Lucero when he turned to face you because he was under that streetlamp down there near the cross street?"

"That's right," confirmed DeRose.

Shaking his head slowly, Bryce commented, "Something's been picking at the back of my brain ever since I came on the scene of the shooting—and it didn't surface until a few minutes ago." He paused a moment, then asked, "If Tony intended to shoot the marshal, why didn't he pick a time and place when there would be no witnesses? I mean, not only could you two gentlemen see him clearly because of where he was standing, he could obviously see you just as clearly because of where *you* were standing."

"Maybe he didn't bother to look in their direction," offered Abe.

"I don't buy that," argued the federal man. "If you were going to gun a man down, wouldn't you look around to make sure there were no witnesses?"

"Well, yeah," the big man admitted, "but who knows what was going through Lucero's mind at the time. Maybe he wasn't even thinking rationally. He's had five years to sit down there in that prison at Santa Fe and let his hatred for my brother grow deeper."

"I don't think so," insisted Bryce. "If Tony had been that far gone with hate, it would have been obvious just by looking at him. Yet I've heard nothing of the sort from anyone who saw him today."

Weston DeRose rubbed his eyes and pinched the bridge of his nose. "What you are saying, then, Bryce, is that you don't think Tony did the killing."

"I'm saying that's a strong possibility," replied the marshal. "It's possible that someone else fired those shots—someone who was standing behind Tony and hit Marshal Washburn in the back, making it look like Tony did it."

"But he had his gun out when Arthur and I saw him," reminded DeRose.

"He could have drawn it when the shots went past him. That would be the natural thing to do. It would have taken you and Mr. Wellman at least a second or two to look in that direction. Right?"

"Well, yes, but—"

"Aw, the kid's guilty and we all know it. All of this is nonsense," came Harold Bentley's sour voice. He got awkwardly to his feet, rubbing his jaw.

"Nonsense?" Bryce echoed as he turned toward Bentley. "I ask again, would a man planning to commit a murder on a public street that is lined with street-lamps not check for witnesses before he drew his gun and fired? There is no way Tony could have overlooked these two men."

Bentley stubbornly snapped, "Well, I agree with Abe. Tony came here so full of hate that he just grabbed his first opportunity to kill Dan without even thinking. He's guilty."

Running his gaze over the faces of the men surrounding him, Bryce asked, "How many of you fellas are planning to ride in the posse?"

Nine hands were raised, including those of Harold Bentley and Abe Washburn.

"Okay," Bryce said, nodding. "Now, of you men, how many agree that there's a possibility Tony Lucero did not kill Dan Washburn?"

Only Bentley's and Abe's hands were not raised. Staring hard at the two dissenters, Bryce told them, "You two will not be riding in the posse." When the men began to protest vehemently, the federal man barked, "Hold it! I will not lead a pack of bloodhounds. Bentley, I don't need an itchy trigger finger in my posse, and that's final, so don't say any more. And Abe, you're just too personally involved. I can't run the risk of you letting your emotions take control of your head if you should spot Tony first when we corner him. If I'm to lead the posse, I insist that you stay here."

The blacksmith seemed ready to object fervidly, but he remained silent.

Bryce informed the rest of the men that they would meet in front of the marshal's office at dawn. "When we catch Tony, we'll find out the truth."

Darlene and Lisa Washburn sat in numb disbelief. When Bob and Dave had first told them about Dan's murder, the two women nearly collapsed from shock. Breaking down and sobbing, Lisa and her mother had held each other tight, each trying to console the other. Now, after their initial outpouring of grief, it was hard for Dan Washburn's wife and daughter really to comprehend the tragic reality of what had happened.

"Dan always told me that I had to be prepared for this day, that there was always the possibility that he would be killed in the line of duty," Darlene finally murmured. "He had warned me about that before he first took the marshal's job back in Pampa. He asked me then if I was sure that I would be able to handle being a lawman's wife, that it would take a certain kind of strength to live constantly with the possibility that he would die from some outlaw's bullet. But I never expected this: murdered in cold blood, shot in the back by some coward seeking revenge. Dan was far too good a man to have died so senselessly."

Sniffling, Lisa said bitterly, "I can't believe that I was happy for Tony Lucero that he was paroled early."

Dave sat down beside his sister. "Don't worry," he told her, his voice cracking. "He'll pay for what he's done—and pay good."

Sunday morning dawned with a clear sky, and Ben Bryce was surprised to find fifteen men gathered in front of the marshal's office. Word of the pursuit of Tony Lucero had apparently spread quickly, and the federal lawman would have to take a chance that all these men were levelheaded.

Bryce briefed them on how the pursuit would be conducted, and he was about to have them mount up when he saw Manuel Lucero cantering along the street. Drawing to a halt, Manuel slid from his saddle and asked if he could ride with the posse, saying he was concerned for the safety of his son.

"Sure, Mr. Lucero. You've certainly got as much right as anyone to be present when your son is apprehended."

"Gracias, señor."

Bryce told the men to mount their horses, and they followed his orders. Just as he was about to do likewise, Bob, Dave, and Abe Washburn galloped up, armed and ready to travel. The marshal felt his stomach muscles tighten, knowing a confrontation was imminent.

Reining in, Bob Washburn looked down at the federal man and told him, "Marshal, we want to be part of the posse. I know what you told Uncle Abe about being too personally involved, but we've a right to be part of the posse."

Peering intently at each of the three men, Ben Bryce argued, "A posse is no place for men who might lose control of their good senses. Lives will be at stake here. I can't let you do it."

Abe shot a glance at Manuel Lucero and said to Bryce, "Is he going?"

"Yes, but—"

"But nothing! Don't tell me he's not emotionally involved!"

"He isn't about to pull a trigger unnecessarily, Mr. Washburn. The hunted man is his son," Bryce pointed out, his voice cool.

"The dead man is my brother," the big man remarked just as coolly. "And he's the father of these two boys. If Manuel goes, we go. Let's be fair about this."

The U.S. marshal sighed, blowing the air out through pursed lips. "All right. But you're to strictly obey my orders. Got it?"

The threesome assured the lawman they would give him no trouble.

Bryce reached for his saddle horn, about to haul himself onto his horse, when Lisa Washburn came from around the corner. Wearing a light shawl thrown over her gingham dress to ward off the morning chill, she came up beside her brother Bob's horse and looked up at him through eyes swollen from crying. "I just wanted to wish you good luck in apprehending Dad's murderer. I just wish I could be there when you capture Tony," she declared hotly.

Ben Bryce lead his horse beside Lisa, then told her, "I understand how you feel, losing your father to a killer's bullets, but—"

"To Tony Lucero's bullets," she corrected him, her eyes flashing with anger.

"Lisa, I know it looks as if Tony is responsible for your father's death, but I've learned that sometimes things are not as they initially seem. Some things have surfaced that leave some doubt."

"How could that be?" she demanded.

"We can talk more about it later. Besides, it's not up to

us to decide Tony's guilt or innocence. A jury will do that."

Looking up at the handsome marshal, Lisa smiled sadly and admitted, "You're right. I guess I'm letting sadness and anger rule my head. It's . . . it's just that I miss my father so much. It's so hard for me to believe that he won't be coming back. I keep thinking he's just gone over to some ranch and that he'll be back shortly . . . and then I remember." She began to cry softly, and Bryce put a consoling arm around her shoulder.

"I'd do anything to take the pain for you," he whispered.

Sniffling, she looked deep into his eyes and murmured, "Thank you."

Releasing her, Bryce mounted his horse and guided the animal to the head of the posse, where Deputy Ned Mills waited. While Mills watched with envy, Lisa told Bryce, "Be careful."

"I will," he assured her with a smile.

As the posse rode out, she stood in the middle of the street, watching. Ben Bryce looked back over his shoulder at the beautiful young woman and felt his heart glow with warmth. There was no question about it. United States Marshal Ben Bryce was falling in love.

Just before dawn, with the stars overhead fading as the light came up, Tony Lucero lay hiding in a brush-covered ravine. Less than five miles from Raton, Tony had spent a sleepless night. Staring up at the lightening sky, he thought how his whole life had crumbled in a matter of minutes.

Everything wonderful that had happened—Dolores's coming back to him, a good job, a welcome home from at least some of the people—was now all taken away from him. It would never be possible to clear himself, for in the eyes of the town he was guilty—and that would never change. If they caught him, they would hang him. His biggest concern, though, was for Dolores.

He knew she had been shot, but he had no idea how seriously.

Broken sobs suddenly wracked his body. How could all of these horrible things have happened in one fell swoop? How could a man's life fall apart so fast? Finally composing himself, he decided that despite the danger, he must return to Raton and find out about Dolores—and he must do it without being caught. He decided to wait the day out in the ravine, then return to Raton under cover of darkness. He would go to Flora Domingo's house, for Flora would know about her niece.

Rising to his feet, young Lucero looked around and satisfied himself that he and the horse were well-hidden in the ravine. He had ridden into it on a rock base several hundred yards away, leaving no hoofprints. It would take an experienced tracker to find him, and there would not be anyone like that in the posse that was sure to come after him. With his mind settled, he lay down again, giving in to the weariness that claimed him, and fell asleep just as dawn broke.

About an hour after the posse left Raton, Juan Gomez knocked on Dr. John Townsend's office door. The burly Mexican heard the sound of footsteps after a moment or two, and then the door came open.

The physician stood there, holding a roll of bandage in his hand. "Hello, Juan," he said in a voice heavy with fatigue. "What can I do for you?"

Speaking quietly, Juan said, "I have come to check on Dolores, Doctor. As you know, I live a couple of miles out of town, and so I just learned of last night's tragedies. I would like to see her, if I may."

Nodding, the physician responded, "Of course. However, I want you to know just how serious her wound is." He explained what had happened to the young woman, adding, "Dolores knows that she will never walk again, yet she is showing great courage."

Juan's face showed the shock he was feeling. He was

silent for a long moment, then finally stammered, "Is . . . is she in pain?"

Townsend shook his head. "No. When the spinal cord was severed, all sensation ceased." With a sigh he took the burly Mexican's arm and said, "Come."

As Juan approached her bed, the dark-eyed beauty smiled weakly.

"Buenos días," he said softly.

"Buenos días, Juan," she responded, her words barely audible. "Did . . . did the doctor tell you I am paralyzed? That I will never walk again?"

Juan bit his lip and nodded silently. Then he murmured, "I want you to know that I still love you and want to marry you."

Dolores closed her eyes, and tears coursed down her cheeks. Opening her eyes again and looking at him, she responded, "I appreciate your kindness, Juan, but I am more concerned about Tony. Has there been any word about him?"

Juan's face hardened. "I have heard nothing," he replied flatly. "Maybe you should not concern yourself so much for him. Maybe he will not want you, now that you are an invalid."

The young woman looked away, although it was clear from her expression that the same thought had occurred to her. Facing Juan again, she replied defensively, "Tony's love for me is real, Juan. My being crippled will not make a difference in how he feels."

Juan started to speak, but he held his tongue. Leaning down, he planted a kiss on Dolores's forehead and remarked, "I know it is tiring for you to have company for too long, so I will go now. I will see you tomorrow."

Dolores reached up and wiped the tears from her cheeks. "Thank you for coming."

Turning sharply on his heels, the husky Mexican walked across the room and left, cursing Tony Lucero under his breath.

Chapter Nine

The voice calling Tony Lucero's name seemed to come from the depths of a deep, distant canyon. Then suddenly a strong hand jarred his shoulder, and he opened his eyes, blinking against the harsh sunlight. The young Mexican sat up and came fully awake, immediately aware of a band of men standing before him. Instinctively his right hand went to his holster, but the gun was gone.

Several of the men who stood looking down at Tony Lucero with hard expressions were holding weapons on him—revolvers and rifles. Shading his eyes, he focused on the faces of the men, and his heart leapt when he saw his father. Just as he was about to speak to Manuel, a man wearing a U.S. marshal's badge ordered, "On your feet, Tony." It was the same voice that had awakened him.

Manuel Lucero stepped beside his son and embraced him when Tony stood up. "Tony," he said with a quiver in his voice, "I know you didn't kill Marshal Washburn. This is United States Marshal Ben Bryce, and he promised me that you will get a fair trial."

Looking at Bryce, Tony stated evenly, "I did not shoot Dan Washburn, Marshal. I know it looks like it, and the whole town thinks it is so, but I am innocent."

"You're a liar, Lucero!" roared Abe Washburn. "Arthur Wellman and Weston DeRose both saw you do it!

Why don't you just come clean and admit you put two bullets in my brother's back?"

Ben Bryce scowled at Abe and snapped, "I told you to keep a cool head, Washburn! Now, back off and keep your mouth shut!"

Another man jumped to the blacksmith's defense. "You don't have the right to speak to Abe that way, Marshal!"

The lawman looked the burly man up and down. "And just who are you?"

"Manfred Jones. I'm the town hostler—not that it makes any difference—and Dan Washburn was my close friend. The way I see it, lawman, you're treating this murderer better than the kin of the man he murdered!" It was clear by the look in Jones's eyes that he was ready for some vengeance of his own. Full of suppressed fury, he stepped close to young Lucero, jabbing a finger at him, and railed, "You're a murderer, all right, and I can't wait to see you swinging at the end of a rope!"

Tony ignored the hostler as best he could, instead turning to his father and asking, "Papa, what about Dolores? Is she all right?"

Manuel's face stiffened. "She is alive, son," he replied. "But she is bad. Very bad."

Ben Bryce pulled a pair of handcuffs from his belt and told the young man, "Let's have your wrists, Tony."

Young Lucero extended his wrists obediently, but his attention was on Manuel. "Papa, what do you mean, she is very bad?"

The ratchets clicked as the handcuffs locked around Tony's wrists. "Your young lady is paralyzed, Tony," Bryce answered solemnly for Manuel, who was clearly unable to utter the words.

Tony was horror-struck. "Paralyzed?"

"Yes. A bullet severed her spinal cord. Dr. Townsend says Dolores will never walk again."

His legs weakening, Tony crumpled to his knees.

"Oh, no!" he gasped, his voice catching in his throat. Lifting his shackled hands up to his face, he cried in anguish, "It's all my fault! It's all my fault! If I hadn't gone to her—" Tony Lucero's words became incoherent.

Manuel stood next to his son, his hand on his shoulder, while the young man wept. After a few minutes the wracking sobs subsided, and Tony looked up at his father. Manuel pulled a bandanna from his hip pocket and gave it to Tony, who wiped his face and blew his nose, then stuffed the bandanna in a pants pocket. "Papa, I need to see Dolores," he declared.

"You can see her as soon as we get back to town, Tony," Bryce said kindly.

Manfred Jones's face went red with fury. "What are you talking about, Bryce! This killer has no right to visit his girlfriend! He's a prisoner, remember?" Looking around at some of the other men, he then shouted, "Maybe we shouldn't bother taking him back to town! Let's string him up right here!"

Many of the men started jeering and hooting in agreement, and the ravine rang with the din of voices clamoring for immediate justice. The federal man could see that it would not take much for these men to get out of control, and he glanced uneasily at Ned Mills, who stood a few feet away, fear written all over him. "Mills!" blurted Bryce. "Let's take charge here!" The federal lawman knew he had to get tough and would need backing up, but the town's deputy seemed rooted to the spot by cowardice and lent no support.

Jones was screaming for a lynching, and the men who were in agreement with him were getting more aggressive by the second. Bryce cut off the hostler's swearing by pointing a stiff finger in his face and shouting, "That's enough, mister!"

Manfred Jones took two steps back, wiping saliva from his mouth. "You're only one man, Marshal," he hissed, "and it's time things were done right around here! We're gonna string this killer up!"

Glancing at the deputy, Ben Bryce saw that Ned Mills was still frozen with fear, and it was plain that he was not going to be of any help. Then, to the federal man's surprise and relief, Abe Washburn and his two nephews began backing him up, trying to calm down the troublemakers. Confident that with the help of the Washburns he could keep the situation from boiling over, Bryce lanced Jones with an ominous look and growled, "You'll have to go through me to string Tony up!"

Jones was beyond reason with rage. He reacted quickly to the lawman's words by swearing and clawing for his weapon—but before his gun cleared the holster, the barrel of Ben Bryce's Colt .45 was leveled between his eyes, hammer cocked. Jones immediately checked his hand, sweat suddenly beading up on his brow.

As all eyes stared at the combatants, the marshal glared at the hostler and challenged through tight lips, "Go ahead, mister, lift that revolver out."

Jones's mouth sagged and he let go of the gun as if it had suddenly turned red-hot.

Holding his gaze hard, Bryce snapped, "I said lift that weapon out of the holster!"

Trembling, Jones bleated, "No, sir, Marshal! I'm not drawing against you!"

"I didn't tell you to draw, mister, I said *lift* it out nice and easy, 'cause I'm taking your gun. It's my job to see that Tony Lucero reaches town safely and that he's given a fair trial. You seem to have other ideas, so I'm taking your weapon."

One of the men who had been stirring up the ruckus called, "Aw, now, c'mon, Marshal. There ain't no reason to—"

"Butt out!" roared the blacksmith, clamping a powerful hand on the man's shoulder. "Let the marshal do his job."

Wincing under Abe's grip, the man stepped back among his cronies.

Ben Bryce glanced over his shoulder as he took Jones's gun from him. "Thanks, Abe. I appreciate your help." Jamming Manfred Jones's revolver under his belt, the federal marshal then ordered, "All right, you men. Let's get our horses and head back to town." As they all made their way out of the ravine, Bryce turned and gave the deputy an icy glare.

Ned Mills looked away, unable to meet the marshal's harsh gaze.

Reaching their horses, everyone mounted up. The deputy rode behind Ben Bryce, next to Abe Washburn, while Tony Lucero rode between his father and the marshal. As they pulled out of the ravine, Tony turned to the federal man and asked, "Marshal, how did you find me? I thought I was well hidden."

Bryce gave him a tight smile and replied, "My job is hunting down men, Tony—and I've had a lot of practice."

When the posse arrived back in Raton, Ben Bryce thanked all the volunteers for their help and informed them that he and Ned Mills would be able to handle matters, so their presence was no longer necessary. The two lawmen and their prisoner—along with Manuel Lucero—had gone barely a block when a man on the street informed them that Clarence Moon had died. Tony Lucero's heart sank, and he turned to Ben Bryce and asked in a frightened voice, "Will I now be tried for two murders, Marshal?"

Shaking his head, Bryce declared, "You shot back in self-defense. No one could call that murder. Besides, the men who pursued you had no authority to do so—and they literally stood in the way of your turning yourself in to the law."

As they headed farther down Main Street, passersby stopped and stared at them, with nearly everyone looking with loathing at the young Mexican. He kept his eyes cast down, despairing that the citizens of Raton had decided his guilt before he had even been tried. With a sigh he turned to Ben Bryce and queried, "Did you mean what you promised before, Marshal? I mean, about stopping at the clinic so I can see Dolores?"

"I gave you my word, Tony. We'll first go to Townsend's place, and then we'll go to the jail."

Ned Mills suddenly protested, "Wait just a darn minute, Bryce. I insist that Tony be jailed immediately. He has no right to see Dolores."

Bryce slowly turned his head toward the deputy, and his face was filled with anger. "Your cowardice nearly cost this man his life, Deputy," the marshal snapped with barely controlled fury. "I'll take responsibility for him from here on out."

Clearly knowing better than to buck the federal man, Mills sullenly backed off. As they passed the marshal's office, the deputy reined his horse in and mumbled that he had work to do, then spurred his mount over to the hitch rail. The other three men continued on without him.

Just before they reached the clinic, Manuel Lucero told his son he would return to town and see him later. Right now, he needed to go home and tell Tony's mother and sisters what had happened.

As the marshal and his prisoner drew up to the doctor's office, Tony felt his body go cold all over. He dreaded seeing Dolores, feeling that he was responsible for her being crippled the rest of her life. He dismounted, and with a heavy heart he moved up the walkway as though he were in a nightmare. His feet felt like lead, yet his knees were so weak they could barely hold him up.

They entered the clinic, and Tony was led in to the young woman by Dr. Townsend. He had thought of dozens of things to say to her, but now that he was standing beside her bed, he could only look down at her in silence, unable to speak.

"Tony," Dolores whispered. "Thank God, you're unharmed! I have been praying that you were all right."

Unable to hold his tears in check, Tony put his hands up to his face and sobbed. Finally he choked out, "My wonderful Dolores! I am so sorry for what has happened. Can you ever forgive me?"

The beautiful Mexican smiled sadly. "There is nothing to forgive, my dearest. You were not the one who shot me."

"But—"

"Hush!" she commanded gently. "Say no more. I will not hear you make such terrible accusations against yourself." Dolores reached up and stroked his face. "You were on your way to turn yourself in to Deputy Mills, hoping to clear yourself. Just remember, none of this would have happened if Marshal Washburn had not been killed—and you did not kill him."

Tony nodded silently, gripping her left hand.

Dolores then asked softly in a tremulous voice, "Tony, do you still want me?"

"Do I still want you?" he echoed with surprise.

"I can never walk again. I will have to spend the rest of my life in a wheelchair. I cannot be the kind of wife that you deserve."

"Oh, my dearest Dolores, of course I still want you! I love you more than you will ever know. It is I who am not deserving of you. But since God has been generous enough to grant me your love, I must trust that somehow I will be freed so we can be married."

When Dolores began to cry, Tony leaned down and kissed her. Suddenly he felt a hand on his shoulder, and he turned.

"We must be going, Tony," Ben Bryce told him.

Dolores looked up at Bryce and pleaded, "Marshal, you must help my Tony. He is innocent. Please believe that."

Bryce smiled down at her. "I do believe it, Dolores, and I promise I'll do all I can to help him."

Three weeks passed. In that time Marshal Dan Washburn was buried, as was Clarence Moon, and the entire town turned out for the funerals. To Lisa Washburn's delight, U.S. Marshal Ben Bryce stayed on in Raton, having informed the federal office in El Paso of his wound and his need to remain until Tony Lucero's trial was held.

In mid-October the circuit judge arrived by stagecoach and met with the town council and the two lawmen. It was agreed that a jury would be selected the following day, and the trial would be held the day after that.

At nine o'clock in the morning on October 16, Raton's town hall, which was used as the courtroom, was jammed full, and the overflow crowd stood outside in the crisp autumn air. The twelve men who had been selected to serve as jurors filed in and sat down. Tony Lucero was seated at a small table a few feet from the judge's bench, and Deputy Ned Mills stood beside him, looking important. When Judge Wallace M. Chapman entered by a back door, Mills asked all to rise. The crowd took their seats after the judge—a distinguished-looking man of sixty with a thick head of silver hair—was likewise seated behind the bench.

Weston DeRose was the first witness, testifying that he had seen Tony Lucero—gun in hand—standing over the crumpled form of Marshal Dan Washburn after two shots were fired. Arthur Wellman followed on the witness stand, and his testimony corroborated DeRose's.

Tony Lucero then gave his side of the story, explaining that the shots came from behind him, just missing his right ear. When the young Mexican's testimony was finished, he returned to the small table and sat down, his head bent. Ben Bryce then testified to the fact that he found it hard to believe that if Tony Lucero had in fact wanted to shoot Dan Washburn, he would not have chosen a more propitious time and place—one that would not put him within clear sight of witnesses. He also stated that neither of the two witnesses ever mentioned having seen smoke issuing from Tony's gun, casting further doubt to his experienced eyes that the young man was the killer.

There was an immediate buzzing through the courtroom, and the faces of the jury showed that Ben Bryce had stimulated their thinking.

Suddenly Manfred Jones was on his feet shouting, "That's just a bunch of hogwash! Gunsmoke would be almost impossible to see from that distance, especially at night!"

The judge banged the desk with his gavel, commanding Jones to sit down and be quiet, but the hostler kept on, saying loudly, "When a man wants to kill somebody bad enough, he doesn't care who's watching! Remember Leo Dunn? He killed George Todd in the bank without batting an eye, and there were plenty of witnesses!"

When the hostler continued to ignore the judge's warning to sit down and be quiet, Ben Bryce leapt from his witness chair and grabbed Jones by the arm, then dragged him from the room. When the lawman returned to the courtroom, the judge asked him if he had anything further to add. Saying he did not, Bryce went back to his chair beside Dolores Domingo, who was seated in a wheelchair.

The jury finally retired to discuss the evidence, and the judge left the room as well, closeting himself in a small anteroom. Tony Lucero sat stony-faced, staring straight ahead while all around him conversations buzzed as to his guilt or innocence.

Barely fifteen minutes later, Judge Wallace M. Chapman reappeared, and the courtroom suddenly went as quiet as a tomb while Chapman took his seat. Then the jury filed in and Chapman asked, "Has the jury reached a verdict?"

Herman Franks, jury foreman, stood up and replied, "We have, Your Honor."

Told to rise and face the jury, Tony Lucero did so, his heart pumping madly and his hands clenched and trembling.

"And what is the verdict?" Chapman asked.

Franks took a deep breath, then replied, "We find the defendant . . . guilty as charged, Your Honor."

Manuel Lucero gasped, while his wife and daughters burst into tears. Dolores Domingo grasped Ben Bryce's arm, and he clasped her hand, shaking his head sadly.

The judge waited until the crowd had quieted down, then looked at Tony and instructed, "Approach the bench for sentencing."

Young Lucero tried to rise, but he was having difficulty standing. Finally Ned Mills gripped Tony's arm and pulled him before the judge.

"Tony Lucero," Chapman intoned, "you have been duly tried by this court of law, and the jury has found you guilty of murder. Do you have anything to say before I pass sentence?"

Tony managed to whisper hoarsely, "I did not do it, Judge. I swear by all that is holy, I did not kill Marshal Washburn."

The judge paused for a moment, then said solemnly, "Mr. Lucero, you have been convicted by this court of murder, and it is my duty to sentence you. Therefore, I hereby sentence you to die by hanging . . . such execution to take place tomorrow morning at sunrise."

Carmen Lucero screamed, her cries echoing off the walls, while Dolores Domingo slumped over in her wheelchair and wept softly.

"I am innocent!" the young Mexican cried. "I am innocent! I did not do it! Please believe me! I did not kill the marshal!"

The judge ignored the defendant and started to rise

to leave. Suddenly Deputy Ned Mills spoke up and informed Chapman that the people of Raton had voted to have no more hangings at the hanging tree, and that a gallows was going to be built by Abe Washburn.

The judge asked if Abe was present, and after the blacksmith identified himself, Chapman then inquired, "How long will the construction take, Mr. Washburn?"

Abe replied, "I'll begin on the gallows immediately—which means I should have it completed in a week."

"Very well," the judge responded. "The execution of Tony Lucero will take place exactly one week from today, October twenty-third, 1887, at sunrise." With that, he banged his gavel once, rose, and hurried out of the building to ride to the next town.

Tony was tearfully embraced by his entire family, then was led through the town hall by Ned Mills. He paused beside Dolores's wheelchair and tried to speak with the young woman, who was being comforted by her aunt, but the angry spectators began threatening the young Mexican. With Ben Bryce hovering closely, making sure that no one approached the condemned man, Mills hurried Tony Lucero out of the building and back to the safety of the jail.

A half hour later Lisa Washburn entered the marshal's office, wanting to discuss the trial with Bryce. From his cell in the rear of the building, the young Mexican recognized Lisa's voice, and he called to her, asking to speak to her for a few moments. Agreeing, Lisa went back to see the prisoner.

Tony stepped to the bars and sorrowfully declared, "Señorita Washburn, I did not kill your father! I swear to you that I am speaking the truth!"

Lisa reached through the bars and touched Tony's arm. "I cannot change the jury's verdict, Tony, but after listening to Ben's arguments, I believe you. I . . . I'm truly sorry that it turned out this way."

The prisoner bowed his head. "Thank you."

Lisa returned to the office and sat down as Ned Mills entered. Sighing deeply, she told the federal man, "You may have heard me just now telling Tony that I believe him, thanks to you, Ben."

Mills took off his hat and tossed it on the desk. Sitting down, he admitted to Bryce, "Your argument convinced me, too. I don't think Tony did it."

Shrugging his shoulders, Bryce remarked, "Which leaves us floundering. If Tony Lucero isn't the murderer, who is?"

Mills suggested that saloon owner Dexter Finn, who had held a grudge against Dan Washburn for running off his customers, might be the guilty party.

"That's right!" Lisa exclaimed. "Remember that recent confrontation between my father and Finn? Why, I remember that Finn's words bordered on a threat." Then shaking her head, she added, "I wonder, though, if he would have gone to that extreme."

Ben Bryce spoke up. "Angry men sometimes do desperate things, Lisa."

Holding up a finger, Mills proposed, "There's another prime suspect."

Bryce and Lisa looked at him searchingly.

"Juan Gomez," came the deputy's response. "He's made no effort to hide his anger toward Tony, and the whole town knows he's as mad as a hornet over losing Dolores. Maybe Juan killed Dan to frame Tony and get him hanged so he could get Dolores back. Killing Tony outright would have put the finger on Juan, but killing Dan would set Tony up perfectly as the apparent killer."

Lisa rubbed her upper arms and shuddered. "This is all so horrible," she murmured. "Here I was feeling a small sense of gratification that at least my father's killer was going to be punished for his crime. Now, though, I feel even more awful. Not only is my father dead, the killer is on the loose."

While dining with Darlene and Lisa Washburn that evening, Ben Bryce told them he was so certain of Tony Lucero's innocence that he planned to wire the circuit judge at his next venue. "I'm going to ask for a postponement of the hanging," he explained, "giving me time to do some investigation. We can't let the real killer get away with it, and we sure can't let Tony hang."

Lisa's eyes lit up for two reasons. With the marshal working on the case, the real killer was bound to be caught—and it meant that the federal man would be staying longer in Raton.

Chapter Ten

During the next few days, as the citizens of Raton passed to and from the north end of town, they would stop with grim interest to watch the gallows taking shape under Abe Washburn's expert hands. The somber structure being erected on the bare, windswept knoll stood out in stark relief against the sky.

By October 20 the platform floor was fitted to the frame, with the square hole for the trapdoor cut out. The platform was ten feet off the ground—thirteen steps up. An eight-by-eight horizontal beam hovering eight feet over the platform would hold the rope that would snuff out the condemned man's life when he plunged through the trapdoor.

On October 22, the day before the hanging was to take place, a reply finally came from Judge Wallace Chapman. To the surprise and disappointment of Ben Bryce, the judge declared that a hunch was not enough evidence for him to grant a postponement of the execution. Without solid evidence to warrant delay, the sentence was to be carried out as ordered.

Heavyhearted, Bryce left the telegraph office and went to the jail to bear the bad news to Tony Lucero. Bryce had discussed his plan with the condemned man after sending the first telegram, getting Tony's hopes up. When the federal marshal gave him the bad news, the young Mexican's whole countenance sagged. Utterly despondent, he sat down heavily on the cot and stared at the floor.

That afternoon Deputy Ned Mills went to the gallows to see whether it had been completed. Reaching the structure, Mills watched as Abe made some final adjustments. The deputy knew it was his job as Raton's only lawman to act as executioner—throwing the lever to release the trapdoor that would plunge the condemned man to his death.

Abe had anchored the hanging rope to the crossbeam and tied a heavy bag of sand to the other end. The bag was lying on the trapdoor with part of the rope coiled on top of it.

"Okay, Ned," said the big, brawny man, "it's all set. The lever is right there under the stairs. All you have to do is give it a good yank. The spring underneath the trapdoor will do the rest. Give it a try."

Mills ran his gaze over the ominous structure. Though the air was cold and a brisk wind was whipping across the knoll, the deputy broke into a sweat.

"What's the matter?" asked Abe.

Mills swallowed hard, then admitted, "Just the sight of this thing gives me the shakes. I don't know if I can pull the lever."

"It's only a bag of sand," the blacksmith reminded him.

"I don't mean I can't pull it now. I mean I don't think I'll be able to pull it when Tony's neck is in the noose."

"If it had been your brother who'd been murdered, I bet you'd find it easy to pull the lever," growled Abe. "I wish I could do it, but it's your job, so you'd better get the feel of it. Yank that lever."

Mills ran a hand slowly over his mouth, then stepped underneath the stairs and gripped the lever. Tensing, he gave the handle a yank. His body jerked as the trapdoor sprung open and the sand bag plummeted, making a heavy *whump* as it fell. As he walked away, his knees weak, Ned Mills dreaded the thought of having to repeat the action the next morning—when Tony Lucero, not a sandbag, would be attached to the end of the rope.

Just before dawn the next morning, Tony Lucero's parents and sisters entered the jail to say their farewells, and Carmen was almost out of her mind with grief. Ben Bryce and Ned Mills led the family to the cell area, and the deputy unlocked Tony's cell door, saying, "I'll let you out of there so you can say a proper good-bye."

Ben Bryce leaned against the doorjamb, weary from barely sleeping the night before. He felt so helpless as he watched Tony embrace his sisters first, then his mother, all of them weeping uncontrollably. Standing beside Manuel, Ned Mills looked away from the Luceros, clearly uncomfortable and sad. Then, without warning, Manuel Lucero snatched the deputy's gun from its holster and rammed the muzzle against Mills's stomach.

Manuel's gun hand trembled as he looked at the U.S. marshal and commanded, "Hand your gun to Tony real easy. Any quick move and the deputy dies!"

Bryce's hands were hanging loosely at his side. Speaking calmly and softly, he suggested, "Manuel, this isn't going to help the situation."

"Oh, yes, it will!" countered Manuel. Glancing at his son, he declared, "Tony, get the marshal's gun, then take it and run! I will hold them here until you are out of town. Go!"

Tony let go of his mother and shook his head. "No, Papa. If I did that, I would have to run for the rest of my life. I would rather die. Tell the marshal and the deputy that you are sorry, and give back the gun."

Hanging his head, Manuel's lips quivered and tears filled his eyes as he handed the weapon back to Ned Mills. Tony threw his arms around his father, and while

Manuel sobbed, the young Mexican's dark eyes focused on Ben Bryce. "Please do not punish him, Marshal."

The lawman stepped closer, then replied, "I won't, Tony. I know he's not thinking clearly right now. I might have done the same thing if I were in his shoes."

Tony thanked Bryce wordlessly by the grateful look in his eyes.

Ben Bryce glanced out the cell window and saw that it was growing lighter. Clearing his throat, he murmured, "It's time to go."

Manuel hugged his son tighter for a moment, then released him. Turning away, he caught Bryce's eye and breathed, "I am sorry, Marshal. Please forgive me."

Bryce laid a firm hand on his shoulder and said, "It never happened, Manuel."

As Tony Lucero was led outside with his hands cuffed in front of him, his weeping family climbed into their wagon and drove east out of town toward home. They could not bear to watch the hanging. Tony watched the wagon for a few moments, then turned in the opposite direction. He stopped short before taking a single step. Just beyond the marshal's office, waiting in her wheelchair with her aunt beside her, was Dolores Domingo.

Tony looked over his shoulder at Ben Bryce, his eyes pleading.

"Go ahead," Bryce told him.

The condemned man moved to the woman he loved and knelt before her. He took her hands in his and whispered, "I just want to look at you one last time."

The dark-haired beauty began to cry—great wrenching sobs that shook her whole body. When her weeping finally subsided, Tony lifted his hands and gently wiped away her tears. Rising, he leaned toward her and kissed her lips. "I love you, my sweet," he told her softly. "My love will always be with you." He kissed her again, then quickly strode away. The two lawmen had to hurry to catch up with him as he walked northward.

Watching the scene from between two buildings was

Juan Gomez. As the two lawmen walked Tony up the street, he followed at a distance, finally slipping away and joining the crowd of townspeople who were heading toward the gallows.

The two lawmen and their prisoner reached the knoll and paused a few yards from the ominous structure. Suddenly young Lucero's knees turned rubbery, and Bryce and Mills had to grab his arms to prevent him from falling. Half carrying Tony, the lawmen moved ahead toward the gallows.

Abe Washburn stood beside his creation and glared at the condemned man. When the threesome drew up to the gallows, the huge man regarded Tony with disdain and sneered, "There are thirteen steps up to the top, murderer. As you step on each one, think of the bullets you put in my brother's back." Tony's face was a mask of terror as he slowly mounted the scaffold, his eyes glued on the hangman's noose swaying menacingly in the breeze. Ben Bryce was immediately behind him, a black hood tucked under his belt.

Tony was halfway up the stairs when his legs gave way again, and his knees cracked loudly against the step as he fell. Ben Bryce gripped him under the arms and helped him to his feet, assisting him the rest of the way to the platform.

Bryce's heart was heavy as he positioned the condemned man on the trapdoor. A wave of nausea swept over the federal man as Tony pleaded, "Help me, Marshal! I am innocent! You believe that I did not kill Dan Washburn! Please do something to help me! Please do not let me die!"

Feeling sickened to his core, Bryce could only murmur, "Forgive me, Tony. I'm so sorry, but there's nothing I can do." Pulling out the hood, he dropped it over the prisoner's head. Then he reluctantly put the noose around the young man's neck. Tony began to whimper, but the sound was muffled by the thick black fabric.

The U.S. marshal gave Tony Lucero one last glance, then descended the steps.

Tony began to wail, and his cries were echoed by Dolores Domingo. The beautiful young woman sat slumped in her wheelchair, her agony all too apparent.

As Ben Bryce reached the ground, he looked over at Ned Mills, who was standing beside the lever, and nodded—but the deputy did nothing. A heavy silence fell over the crowd, and all eyes were riveted on Mills as they waited for him to perform his duty. But, his body seemingly frozen except for the trembling hand gripping the lever, Ned Mills did not move.

Ben Bryce looked up at Tony Lucero, who was weeping and mumbling, his body quaking uncontrollably, and then his eyes swept over the expectant, hushed crowd. Taking a step toward the deputy, the federal man hissed at Mills through clenched teeth, "Pull it!"

The deputy swallowed and shook his head. He drew a shuddering breath and said hoarsely, "I . . . I can't. I can't kill an innocent man."

Abe Washburn, who was standing a few feet away, heard the exchange. He swore and moved toward Mills, blurting, "Get out of the way! I'll gladly pull it!"

Bryce darted into Abe's path and warned, "You pull that lever, and I'll arrest you for murder!"

"What are you talking about?" asked Abe gruffly. "The execution has got to be carried out!"

"Only by proper authority!" Bryce retorted. "A lawman is authorized by society to be an executioner. If anyone else pulls that lever, it's murder, not execution. Ned Mills is Raton's only legal lawman; therefore, he must be the one to pull the lever."

Tony Lucero suddenly cried out, "You are hanging the wrong man! Please do not go through with this!"

Everyone in the crowd stared wide-eyed as Abe Washburn and Ben Bryce argued. Suddenly the big man shouted, "Then *you* pull the lever, Bryce!"

"I can't," replied Bryce. "My badge gives me authority in federal matters, not local ones."

The bizarre delay of the execution was beginning to take its toll. With the condemned man's screams hanging heavily in the air, many of the onlookers began looking queasy, while others were almost in shock. One man was heard to mutter, "I thought this here gallows was gonna make things easier."

Suddenly Weston DeRose rushed up to Ned Mills, swearing at him heatedly. "Do your duty and yank that lever, Mills! Now!"

The deputy stood like a statue, his right hand still gripping the lever. Abruptly he let go of it and mumbled, "I can't do it. I just can't do it."

DeRose reached out and ripped the badge from Mills's chest. "If you aren't going to perform the duties of your office," the council chairman spat, "you will not wear this badge." Pivoting, he confronted Ben Bryce. "I'll swear you in right now as marshal of Raton. Then you can pull the lever."

Bryce shook his head. "I can't be sworn in as a lawman anywhere unless I first resign as a United States marshal—and there's no time for that." He glanced up at the top of the platform, then back at DeRose. "Look," he said in a low voice, "if that lever isn't pulled, we've got to get Tony off the gallows and back to his cell. Making him wait up there is cruel and unusual punishment—and the Bill of Rights frowns on that kind of treatment."

"Why not deputize me?" Abe Washburn put in. "Then we can get this thing over with."

Spinning around, DeRose stared at Abe. Tony's horrifying wails distracted him for a moment, but then the councilman nodded his head. He told the big man to raise his right hand, then swore him in. As soon as he had pinned the deputy's badge on the blacksmith's jacket, he ordered, "Do it! Hurry!"

Tony Lucero's heartrending cry was echoing across

the hills as Abe Washburn, a triumphant look on his face, stepped up to the lever and quickly threw it. The trapdoor gave way, and Tony Lucero plunged to his death.

Relieved that young Lucero at least died instantly once the lever was thrown, the crowd began to disperse slowly. It was obvious, though, from the expressions on their faces and the stiffness of their walks, that the onlookers were numb from the horrible experience. Abe Washburn removed the badge from his chest, handed it back to Weston DeRose, and stated, "I resign." As he walked past Ned Mills, heading for the Washburn family somberly standing nearby, Abe shook his head wordlessly and growled, "You're the poorest excuse for a lawman I've ever seen. My brother must be rolling over in his grave."

Turning away from Abe, Mills saw the scorn in the eyes of the people around him. It was obvious that he had lost their confidence, and without a word to anyone he walked away. He would pick up his belongings at his boardinghouse, then ride out of Raton for good.

Weston DeRose watched the former deputy leave, then turned to Ben Bryce and asked, "Is there any way you can become our marshal until a new one can be found?"

Bryce answered, "Well, I'll wire the federal office in El Paso and ask for an official leave of absence. If they approve, then I'll do it."

Overhearing the conversation, Lisa Washburn smiled, elated that Ben Bryce would be around still longer.

The next day the El Paso office wired approval of Ben Bryce's leave of absence, allowing him legally to be sworn in as marshal of Raton. He was to report back to El Paso for reinstatement as U.S. marshal as soon as possible.

The town council gathered at the marshal's office for

the swearing in. After pinning the marshal's badge on Bryce's chest, Weston DeRose shook his hand and said with a smile, "I think we just won't look for another man, Ben. Maybe we'll just keep you for our marshal."

The others all laughingly agreed, and Bryce thanked them for their confidence but assured them he would be returning to his federal job. They had best begin looking for another marshal right away.

As the councilmen headed for the door, Bryce called, "Gentlemen, before you go, I would like to talk to you about Tony Lucero."

Eyebrows were raised. "What about him?" asked DeRose.

"I believe an innocent man was wrongly hanged."

There was a collective gasp from the seven council members.

"Are you sure?" Herman Franks asked.

"Yes." Bryce then told them what he and Ned Mills had discussed, explaining that he had even gone so far as to wire Judge Chapman for a postponement of the execution but was refused.

Weston DeRose said, "Ben, I realize Tony declared his innocence right up until the end, and I have thought over the arguments you gave that day in court . . . but do you have something else that convinces you beyond a shadow of a doubt that he was innocent?"

"Not really," the marshal admitted. "But my arguments were valid—I believe sufficiently so to have warranted further investigation before the trial was concluded. Unfortunately, Judge Chapman didn't agree with me."

DeRose sighed, "No wonder Ned Mills was unable to pull that lever. If I'd been in his shoes, I don't think I would have behaved any differently."

Dave Washburn spoke up. "Ben, if you're correct and Tony really was innocent, then—"

"—then the real killer got away with murdering your dad and is walking free in Raton," the marshal concluded. He paused, adding, "And Tony Lucero died in his place."

"Okay," put in Bob Washburn, "let's say you're right. Then who could it be . . . and why would he want to kill Dad?"

Reluctant to tip his hand, Ben Bryce did not reveal his suspicions about Juan Gomez and Dexter Finn. But he would keep a close watch on both men, studying their routines and casually asking questions around town about them. It would take some time, but if he began to suspect one man more than the other, he would apply some subtle pressure and see what developed. Finally answering Bob Washburn's question, he said, "I don't know who, Bob, and there's no way to know why until I've got the guilty man in custody. But I promise you this: I'm going to do everything I can to find out."

Edgar Willows's face paled. Running a shaky hand over his eyes, he breathed, "Gentlemen, I sat on that jury, and I was sure we had the right man. Oh, how awful if we were wrong! That would haunt me for the rest of my days!"

Weston DeRose rubbed the back of his neck. "The whole town will feel the guilt, Edgar. In essence, we all voted to hang Tony."

"There is no way to bring Tony back," Bryce reminded them, his voice heated, "but I'm going to do my best to clear his name. Somebody in this town wanted Dan Washburn dead and used Tony Lucero's old threat to kill Dan and let Tony pay for it. I intend to make sure that Dan's *real* murderer pays for his crime."

On the following Sunday afternoon a brilliant sun warmed the high New Mexico countryside. Bob Washburn decided to take his wife and children for a ride to the crest of Raton Pass, for it would probably be the last opportunity to do so before the snow came. He also hoped the ride would cheer them up a bit.

Bundled up in coats, the family climbed into their

buckboard behind the two-horse team and headed north toward the pass. As they meandered along the winding road that in some places ran right along the edge of the mountain they were unaware that a lone rider was following them, keeping well back and out of sight. Soon the Washburns were nearing the top of the pass, and the team pressed hard into the harness to pull the wagon up the dusty incline.

Four-year-old Danny sat beside his father on the front seat, and little Mary Jane held her mother's hand on the rear seat. Danny leaned close to his father and advised, "Daddy, don't drive too close to the edge. It's a long way to the bottom."

From behind him Patty laughed. "Don't worry, honey. Your daddy wouldn't put us in any danger. He just wants us to enjoy the beauty of the canyon."

They topped the crest, and Bob hauled up to allow his family to take in the view. He commented that they would turn around where the road widened up ahead.

Danny stood up and looked over the edge, his eyes wide with awe. Then he pointed and exclaimed, "Look down there, Daddy! Some people!"

Both parents looked down the narrow, winding road that led to the bottom of the Colorado side of the pass. It took them a few seconds to spot the people Danny was pointing at far below, but they finally focused on a wagon and team just beginning the long climb up. Then the vehicle passed from view when the road curved around the far side of the mountain.

Flicking the reins, Bob started up the team. As they drove along the edge of the sheer cliff, galloping hoofbeats were heard behind them, coming over the crest of the pass. Patty twisted around to see who was approaching, and recognizing the rider, she smiled and raised a hand in greeting. The smile quickly drained away at the sight of the revolver in his hand. The horseman fired twice, hitting Bob in the back and killing him almost instantly, and Patty screamed in horror and disbelief as her husband slumped over in the driver's seat. Startled by the gunshots, the team bolted in fear, and the rider then fired two more shots just above the heads of the horses, frightening them further.

The young mother and her two children clung to the sides of the wagon in terror as it bounded and careened down the steep road behind the galloping team. The road took a sudden turn, and the terrified horses plunged over the edge of the cliff, their feet pawing frantically in midair. As the wagon sailed into the canyon Patty's bloodcurdling screams echoed off the mountainside. Finally, after many seconds, there was silence.

The horseman sat his mount at the edge of the cliff, watching impassively. Then reining his mount around, he smiled and headed back to Raton.

Marshal Ben Bryce stepped out of Judge Wallace M. Chapman's room at the Raton Hotel. The judge was passing through Raton on his way westward, and when Bryce had learned of the judge's presence, he went to see him. Explaining that he had been made marshal until a replacement for Dan Washburn could be found, Bryce told Chapman that he was determined to prove Tony Lucero's innocence before he resumed his duties as a federal marshal.

Leaving the hotel, Bryce was crossing the street to his office when two men in a wagon hauled up in front of him. The driver called to him, noting, "You appear to be the law here."

"That's right," confirmed Bryce with a nod. "Is there something I can do for you?"

The driver cleared his throat and said, "My name's Trendley, George Trendley. Me and my partner are from over Colorado way. Trinidad."

"Uh-huh."

"We were drivin' up the pass headin' for Raton when we saw a team and wagon peel over the edge of the canyon from up near the top of the pass." Curling a thumb over his shoulder, he pointed to the rear of the wagon, which was covered by a canvas tarp. "We recovered four bodies—a man and a woman, and their two kids. At least, what's left of them."

Eyes wide, Ben Bryce grabbed the corner of the tarp and flung it back. His stomach dropped at the sight of the battered, broken bodies of Bob Washburn and his family. Gritting his teeth, Bryce gasped, "Good God! I wonder how on earth it happened!" He shuddered, then breathed, "What a horrible way to die!"

"It was for the woman and the kids, Marshal," the driver agreed, "but the man never knew what hit him." When Bryce looked at him sharply, Trendley explained, "He's got two bullets in his back. Dead center between his shoulders. He was dead before the wagon even left the road, is my guess."

Bryce reached in the bed and rolled Bob Washburn over. "Just like his dad," he muttered to himself.

After leading the wagon to Wilbur Nicely's funeral parlor and depositing the bodies there, Bryce thanked the two men for their help and they headed off. The marshal then went to Abe Washburn's house and informed him of what had happened, asking Abe to accompany him as he broke the news to the rest of the family. The big man appeared stunned, grieved, and angered all at the same time. Agreeing to go with Bryce, he moaned as they walked toward Darlene Washburn's house, "What kind of crazed maniac is killing off my family?" He was silent for a while, then asked, "Ben, do you realize what this means?"

"Yeah. Tony Lucero really *was* innocent."

The blacksmith looked stricken. "Oh, how awful! Tony was telling the truth, and nobody believed him!"

"I did," Bryce retorted.

Reaching the Washburn house, the men broke the dreadful news to Darlene and Lisa. Darlene nearly fainted upon hearing of the death of her son, daughter-in-law, and grandchildren, and Lisa looked as though she were in a complete state of shock. Bryce and the blacksmith helped the two women to the sofa, where they sat in numb disbelief. Then the lawman suggested, "Abe, you stay here, and I'll go tell Dave and Wilma what's happened. I'm sure they'll want to come back here so you can all be together."

When the family was all gathered, they discussed the implication of the deaths. It meant that Tony Lucero had died for a crime he did not commit, and there was a cold-blooded murderer at large. He had killed again—and again he had killed Washburns.

Chapter Eleven

The news about the Washburn murders spread like wildfire through Raton. By the following morning the town was in an uproar when the citizens realized Tony Lucero had been telling the truth when he proclaimed his innocence from the gallows.

Marshal Ben Bryce had been in his office only minutes when Manuel Lucero came through the door, his face anguished. "Is it true, Marshal? Someone has murdered Bob Washburn and his family?"

Bryce rose to his feet. He felt sick inside and could not meet the elderly Mexican's boring gaze. "Yes, Manuel," he sighed, tugging on his mustache, "it's true."

"See?" Manuel cried, choking on the word. "I told everybody my son was innocent! You hanged an innocent, man, Marshal! Do you hear me? My boy was innocent and you hanged him!"

Bryce quickly explained that he had believed Tony was innocent and even tried to get a postponement of the execution, but it had been denied by the judge for lack of evidence. When he heard this, Manuel calmed down slightly, then thanked the lawman for trying to save his son.

Finally meeting the man's sorrow-filled eyes, Bryce told him, "While nothing can bring your son back to you, I promise that I will do everything in my power to bring the real killer to justice and clear Tony's name."

Manuel twisted his hat in his hand and lowered his head. In a barely audible voice he murmured, "I must go home and tell Carmen this news. All of this has been so hard on her that I am afraid—"

The Mexican's words were disrupted by the sound of gunfire, and Ben Bryce charged past Manuel Lucero and bolted outside. More shots were heard, and the marshal determined they were coming from the Lucky Dog Saloon.

Sprinting across the street to the barroom, Bryce dashed onto the boardwalk, and drawing his gun, he elbowed his way through the crush of people gathering near the door. Then, taking a deep breath and preparing himself for action, he burst through the batwing doors. Two men were sprawled on the floor, and most of the patrons were backed up against the far wall. A pair of unkempt drifters stood over the bodies with smoking guns in their hands. The marshal glanced at Dexter Finn, who stood behind the bar, his face white.

Before Bryce could speak, one of the drifters brought his gun to bear on the lawman. But Bryce fired first, drilling the man through the heart. The loud roar of the gun reverberated off the walls as the drifter hit the floor, and the Colt .45's muzzle was immediately trained on the other man.

The second saddle tramp dropped his weapon and threw up his hands, shouting, "Don't shoot, Marshal! I ain't takin' you on!"

While holding his gun on the man—who gave his name as Vernon Kline—Bryce questioned Finn and the patrons about the shootings. The lawman learned that the drifters had been in a poker game with a couple of local young men, neither of whom were armed. Then an argument broke out, and the saddle tramps started shooting, leaving one of the young men dead almost instantly. The other one, though wounded, had tried to fight back with a chair, but the drifters turned on him and shot him dead.

Kline was taken to the jail and locked up. The next day, after the funeral for Bob Washburn and his family, a trial was held, with Judge Chapman presiding. Vernon Kline was convicted of murder within minutes and sentenced to hang at sunrise the following morning.

Heavy clouds covered the sky when dawn broke, and a cold wind whistled through the mountain town. A few people gathered at the gallows to watch the hanging, most of them relatives of the murdered young men. Hats and bonnets pulled low, they scrunched their heads into their coat collars against the wind and fixed their eyes on Vernon Kline as Marshal Bryce escorted him toward the gallows. Accompanying Bryce was Abe Washburn, who had volunteered to help with the execution.

As the men stepped up to the gallows, the drifter began to shake and whimper. His face was devoid of color, and his wide, frightened eyes stared at the instrument of death outlined against the bleak New Mexico sky.

Kline dug his heels in the ground, shaking his head violently. "No! Please don't hang me! Ple-e-e-ease!" He resisted climbing the steps of the gallows with every ounce of strength within him.

Turning his head slightly, Bryce said, "Abe . . ."

Abe Washburn's strength easily defeated the condemned man. He was suddenly propelled up the first step and forced to continue climbing. Shoving him upward, Abe muttered, "Time's a-wasting, mister. We want to get this over with as fast as you killed those two innocent young men."

Vernon Kline sobbed pitifully as Abe covered his head with the black hood. The sobbing grew louder when the rope was tightened around his neck. After making sure the saddle tramp was properly positioned on the trapdoor, the big man descended the thirteen stairs, his ponderous head bent against the biting wind.

Reaching the bottom, he looked over his shoulder at Ben Bryce, who stood beneath the staircase with his hand on the lever, and nodded. "Okay, Marshal."

Bryce worked the lever, and the drifter plummeted to his death.

Abe Washburn looked up at the man's body, swaying in the wind. "Glad to see my gallows is working without a hitch," he declared.

Two days later Dave Washburn locked up his store at closing time, exiting through the back door into the alley, as was his custom. His mind went to Bob, who had come out the same door with him thousands of times over the years. He missed his brother terribly, and the thought of him brought a painful lump to his throat.

It was already dark, the days having shortened with winter's approach, and flakes of snow were falling. Pulling his collar up, Dave tightened his hat on his head and started down the alley toward home, looking forward to the hearty supper Wilma would have waiting for him.

Dave had gone only a few yards when a menacing figure emerged from a hiding place in the alley and came up behind him. Raising his arm, he struck Dave Washburn over the head with a heavy club.

Wilma Washburn, who was nearly seven months pregnant, paced the floor in her kitchen, her pretty face filled with concern. The potatoes were now overcooked, and the gravy was cold and lumpy. Glancing at the clock, she saw that Dave was now more than thirty minutes late. What was keeping him? His work load was heavier with Bob gone, but Wilma knew her husband would send someone to tell her if he were going to be late for supper.

Knowing that someone in town seemed to have it in for the Washburn men, fear scratched at the expectant mother's mind. Would this unknown assailant strike again? Was he only after the Washburn men? It certainly seemed that way. The killer had shot both Dan and Bob, but no bullets were found in the bodies of Patty or the children. They apparently had died simply because they were with Bob.

The strain was too much. Wilma could wait no longer. Removing the apron that covered her enlarged abdomen, she put on her heavy wool coat, wrapped a scarf around her head, and left the house.

Less than ten minutes later Wilma was in the alley rattling the back door of the store. When she found it locked, she pounded on it, calling her husband's name. Getting no response, she went around the building to Main Street and tried the knob on the front door. It was also locked, and there were no lights inside.

Panic was rising in Wilma Washburn as she hurried down the street to the Raton Hotel, where Marshal Ben Bryce was now residing. Snowflakes melted on her coat as she entered the lobby and crossed to the desk.

The night clerk smiled. "Good evening, Mrs. Washburn. What brings you out on a cold night like this?"

Not bothering to answer his question, Wilma glanced at the stairs and asked, "Is Marshal Bryce in his room?"

"No, ma'am. He's over at Mamie's Café eating supper with your husband's uncle."

Thanking the clerk, Wilma dashed out the door and crossed the street to the restaurant. Looking around the crowded room, she spotted Abe Washburn and Ben Bryce seated at a table near the back. Wilma made her way awkwardly among the closely set tables, gasping for breath by the time she reached the two men, who, from the amount of food on the plates in front of them, had obviously just begun eating.

"Wilma! What's the matter?" Abe asked immediately. "I can see that you're upset."

"It's Dave," she replied shakily. "He didn't come home for supper, and I can't find him. I went to the store, but he's not there. It's locked up."

"Did you look inside the store?" queried the marshal, wiping his mouth and mustache with a napkin.

"No. There were no lights inside, so I came to find you." She looked from man to man. "Did either of you see him?" she asked in a small voice.

Both men shook their heads. Abe then answered, "I was heading home myself when I ran into Ben and suggested we have dinner together." He looked at Wilma solicitously and put a comforting hand on her arm. "You have a key to the store, don't you?"

"Yes."

"Let's go."

They hurried to the store, and the two men made a quick search but found no sign of Dave nor any indication that there had been a struggle. Bryce speculated that if something had happened to Dave, it would have been after he left the store. Using lanterns, they looked in the alley behind the store, but the freshly fallen snow showed no footprints.

"Let's go back to your house, Wilma," suggested the lawman. "Maybe Dave's there by now. He might have stopped off somewhere."

"It wouldn't be like him to do that," Wilma maintained, "but I sure hope it's so."

Arriving at the house, they found it empty. Wilma began to tremble and said, shuddering, "Something's happened to him. I just know it!"

Abe took Wilma in his arms and said soothingly, "Now, honey, don't panic. You've got to think of your baby, so you just sit down here and take it easy. I'll run next door and see if Ethel Mitchell has finished feeding her husband and son and can stay with you while the marshal and I round up some men. I promise you we'll search for Dave until we find him."

Clinging to the big man, Wilma tried hard not to cry as she murmured, "Oh, Abe, what if that killer has murdered Dave?"

"Now, hush," he countered gently. "I won't have you

thinking such gruesome thoughts. You'll see. We'll find your errant husband soon. He's probably stopped for a drink, or maybe he ran into somebody who needed a hand with something." He smiled at her encouragingly, then leaving her with Bryce, went next door. He soon returned with the neighbor lady, Ethel Mitchell.

A half hour later, Abe and the marshal had assembled twenty-three men to form a search party. Carrying lanterns and going out in teams of two, the men set forth to search the streets and alleyways of Raton as best they could in the darkness and the falling snow.

At midnight the search party reassembled in front of the marshal's office, having found nothing. Discussing the situation with Ben Bryce, the men all decided that Dave Washburn had undoubtedly met with foul play—just like his father and brother.

Abe Washburn was furious. His face darkening, he demanded, "Ben, you've got to do something. This murdering scum has got to be caught."

Before Bryce could reply, one of the men suggested, "Well, for my money, I think the guilty party is Dexter Finn. We all know that he had it in for Dan. I think he murdered Dan, and now for some crazy reason he's decided to kill off the rest of the men in the Washburn family."

"Well, if you ask me," put in another man, "I think our man is Juan Gomez. He's relatively new here, and what does anyone actually know about him? I mean, he lives out there in that house that belonged to those two old hermits who died a couple of years ago, and he doesn't mingle much with any of us, except for Dolores Domingo. The way I see it, maybe he killed Dan to make it look like Tony did it, removing him as a rival for Dolores, and now he's killing other Washburn men to throw off suspicion."

Weston DeRose set his lantern down next to his feet and countered, "I've been doing some thinking about this, fellas, and I've come up with another angle."

Ben Bryce eyed him in the flickering lantern light and insisted, "Let's hear it, Mr. DeRose. The job of flushing out the killer is on my shoulders, and being a stranger here myself, I can use any angle any one of you can come up with."

"All right," DeRose responded, "tell me what you think of this. How about if we go back to what the jury decreed? Tony killed Dan."

"I don't buy it," replied Bryce, "but go ahead. I'm listening."

"Okay. Let's say Tony really did shoot Dan in the back. And now Manuel Lucero is getting revenge for *his* son's death by killing *Dan's* sons. Patty and the children just happened to be with Bob when Manuel struck."

Ben Bryce rubbed his chin and said, "I still believe Tony was innocent, but since you've raised the possibility that Manuel may have some involvement in these murders, I'll question him as well as the other two men."

"When are you gonna question 'em?" asked Abe.

"First thing in the morning."

"I want to go with you when you do," the blacksmith insisted.

"I don't know," replied Bryce, shaking his head. "You've got a pretty flinty temper, Abe. You got mighty hot when we ran down Tony. Like I've said before, you're too emotionally involved—even more so now, with Bob and his family murdered and perhaps Dave having been murdered, too."

The huge man reasoned with the marshal that he had a right to be present when the suspects were questioned. After all, it was his family that was under attack.

Bryce thought about it for a moment, then relented. "All right, Abe, but you have to keep your temper under control." His pale blue eyes looked intensely at the big man. "Got it?"

"Got it," agreed Abe. "You won't have any problem

from me. Besides, if we're right about one of these guys being the killer, and he decides to fight his way out, I might just come in handy."

Looking the huge man up and down, the marshal chuckled, "You might at that."

"Well," sighed Abe, "I'm going over to Wilma's place. She should have someone in the family with her."

Nodding, Bryce remarked, "Good idea. And tell her that we haven't given up. We'll find Dave." The lawman stared vacantly for a moment, then added softly, "I just hope he's alive when we do."

Lisa Washburn answered the door when Abe knocked. From the expectant look on her face, it was obvious that she had hoped to see the face of her brother. "Oh, Uncle Abe," she breathed, "it's you."

The big blacksmith was equally surprised to see his niece standing there. "Who told you that Dave was missing?"

"Wayne Mitchell—you know, Ethel's son. Ethel thought it would be a good idea for us to be with Wilma, so she sent Wayne over to get us. Besides, it's only right that Mother and I should know about . . . about . . ." The lovely blonde bit down on her lip and her eyes misted. "Did you find Dave?" she finally managed to ask.

"Not a trace," Abe replied glumly.

At that moment Wilma and Darlene emerged from the parlor. Wilma ran to the huge blacksmith and threw her arms around him, crying, "I heard what you just said. Oh, I'm so frightened! I'm afraid I'll never see Dave alive again!"

"Aw, now, honey," Abe rejoined, holding her with one hand and patting her back with the other, "it may not be as bad as we think. You just hold on. Old Abe's gonna stay right here in the house with you tonight and keep you company."

Darlene offered, "That won't be necessary, Abe. Lisa and I can stay with her. We were already planning to."

"Well, then, I'll just stay with the whole bunch of you," Abe said tenderly. "You're my family, and I'm gonna be here in case there's any kind of trouble."

The Washburns all went into the parlor. Ethel Mitchell was sitting on the couch, and she stood up and moved toward Wilma. "Well, I guess I'll be getting on back, my dear. Please let me know if there's anything else I can do for you. And let me know if . . . that is—"

"I understand," Wilma assured her. "And thank you, Ethel."

Wilma walked her neighbor to the door. Ethel was about to leave when she glanced at Abe, who stood watching them. She smiled up at the strapping blacksmith and declared, "I guess with you protecting them, these ladies have nothing to fear from anyone."

Early the next morning Ben Bryce was standing by the washstand in his hotel room, just about to shave, when there was a knock at his door. Holding the straight-edged razor in one hand, he moved to the door, shaving soap dripping from his face.

Opening the door, Bryce recognized two elderly men he had often seen around Raton. He believed they both lived somewhere on the north side of town.

"Marshal!" exclaimed one of the men. "We just found Dave Washburn!"

"Where?" blurted Bryce. "Is he all right?"

"No, he's not all right, Marshal. As a matter of fact . . . well, we was headin' out of town, and we was passin' by the knoll when we looked up and saw Dave up there on that there gallows his uncle built. He's . . . he's hangin' by his neck from a rope."

Bryce dropped the razor and wiped the soap from his face with a towel. He then hurriedly finished dressing and dashed from his room, descended the stairs three at a time, and ran across the lobby, out of the hotel. The lawman sprinted up the street to the north end of town, and by the time he arrived at the gallows, other people had gathered. Coming to a halt at the bottom of the knoll, the federal man stood gasping, and the gulps of icy air hurt his lungs. He looked up at Dave Washburn's body sagging against the rope that was looped over the crossbeam and shuddered. His hands bound behind him, Dave's face was bloated and purple, and his eyes bulged from their sockets.

Wilbur Nicely, the undertaker, was standing at the bottom of the structure, as if to keep anyone from getting near the body. Nicely, who lived at that end of town, nodded grimly at Bryce as he drew beside him and then followed the lawman up the steps. The steps were crusted with a layer of snow, yet there were no footprints except the ones the two men were making. Obviously the killer had done his dastardly work early enough—probably just after Dave closed up the store—so that the snow that fell afterward covered up any telltale prints.

Studying the snow-covered body, Bryce muttered to the undertaker, "Take a look at his face, Wilbur. He was hanged in a way so as to choke to death, not die instantly from a broken neck."

The undertaker paled. "Who would do such a gruesome thing? It's bad enough to murder him—but in such a horrid manner!"

The two men removed the corpse from the noose and laid it on the platform. Examining the body, the lawman noted a knot on the back of the head, indicating that the killer had hit Dave from behind with a blunt instrument. "He must have deliberately waited for Dave to regain consciousness before stringing him up," Bryce pointed out, "then used a sufficiently slack rope to insure a slow death." He rubbed a weary hand over his eyes, then said, "Let's get him down from here."

The lawman and the undertaker carried the body down the steps, and then some of the onlookers helped

Wilbur Nicely carry it to his funeral parlor. Ben Bryce stood watching the men bearing their tragic burden, then, with a heavy heart, made his way to Wilma Washburn's house.

Reaching the small, tidy house, he walked up the steps to the porch and knocked loudly, and after a few moments Abe Washburn opened the door. He was chewing a piece of toast and quickly swallowed it.

"Come in, Ben. I'll be ready in a couple of minutes. I didn't realize you wanted to get such an early start to go question those three. Of course, I guess we have to if we're gonna catch Juan Gomez at home. He probably leaves early on his odd jobs. I assume you want to begin with him."

Closing the door behind him, Ben sighed, "I'm here for another reason, Abe. Is Wilma up?"

"Not yet. Darlene and Lisa came over last night and stayed here, and they gave Wilma some sedative powders that she had on hand. She's still asleep. Come on back to the kitchen. Want some breakfast? Coffee?" The big man started toward the kitchen, then stopped as the somber look on Bryce's face apparently registered. "What is it, Ben?" he asked, his voice concerned. "Have you found Dave?"

"Yeah."

Darlene and Lisa suddenly appeared, and the older woman asked, "Ben, did I hear you say you've found Dave?"

Bryce nodded silently, glanced at Lisa, then looked back at Darlene. He told them the grisly news, wishing he could spare them the horrid details. But knowing they would learn of them anyway, he held nothing back.

Darlene Washburn's body sagged, and Lisa caught her mother and helped her to a chair. Clearly fighting her own grief, Lisa brought her mother a cup of cold water and, kneeling before her, helped Darlene sip it.

Fuming with anger, Abe launched into a furious tirade, promising that soon another man was going to be hanging on the gallows—the killer. He stopped pacing abruptly and looked down at the two women. "I'm sorry," he apologized. "I guess I'm not making it any easier. It's just that I feel so useless and—"

Lisa stood up and patted her uncle's arm. Tears streamed down her face as she murmured, "It's okay, Uncle Abe. We understand. Each of us has a different way of expressing our grief."

The bulky blacksmith embraced his niece. Then he turned to Bryce and demanded, "What are we waiting for? There's a murdering coward out there somewhere, and you and I are gonna find him! I'd like to strangle the life out of him with my own bare hands, but I promise I'll let the law exact justice on him. You ready to go?"

The marshal replied, "Maybe we'd better wait till Wilma wakes up, to give her the news."

"That's all right, Ben," Lisa put in. "I'll tell Wilma. You and Uncle Abe go on and track down the fiend who's doing this to our family."

Bryce stepped to Lisa's side and put his hands on her shoulders. "I'm so sorry," he said gently, gazing into her eyes. "I can't imagine how you're holding up through all this. You're a very strong young woman, Lisa Washburn—and I admire you greatly."

She gave him a tentative smile. "Thank you, Ben. That means a lot to me."

Bryce kissed the lovely blonde on the forehead. "You take good care of yourself. I'll see you later."

Marshal Ben Bryce and Abe Washburn loosened the guns in their holsters as they dismounted in front of Juan Gomez's isolated house. Bryce glanced at the small barn in the back, but there was no way to tell if Juan's horse was inside.

Stepping onto the slightly sagging porch, Bryce felt the boards give under his weight. He knocked loudly on the door, then glanced around at Abe, who waited a few steps back in the yard.

There was no answer. When no response came at his second knock, Bryce walked to the barn and looked inside. Juan's horse was not there. "We'll come back later," he told Abe. "Let's head for Lucero's place."

The lawman felt a bit uncomfortable as he and the blacksmith dismounted at Manuel Lucero's house. He hated having to upset the Luceros any more than they already were—for he was absolutely sure that Manuel was no more guilty of murdering the Washburn brothers than Tony had been of murdering their father. He told Abe, "Frankly, it's unlikely that Manuel is our killer, if for no other reason than he isn't strong enough to have carried Dave up the steps to the top of the gallows, then string him up—unless he had help, which is a ridiculous idea. No, I'm more convinced than ever that Juan Gomez or Dexter Finn is our man."

Before Bryce even knocked, Manuel opened the door, obviously having seen their arrival. The two men were invited to sit down at Lucero's kitchen table, and when they were settled, the marshal looked across at Manuel and explained, "I have a couple of questions to ask you."

Carmen and her daughters stood behind Manuel, and all four were looking at Bryce and Washburn with puzzled expressions. "Questions about what, Marshal?" queried Manuel.

Keeping his voice as nonaccusatory as possible, the marshal said, "Where were you last Sunday afternoon? Say between one and four?"

Manuel's face tightened. "Why?" he asked sharply.

"I need to know, for the record. I also must ask you where you were last evening at suppertime."

Manuel pulled at an ear and said, "Does your question about last Sunday afternoon have anything to do with Bob Washburn and his family being run over the cliff by an unknown killer?"

"Yes."

"And you think I did this terrible thing?" the Mexican asked, shocked and visibly shaken.

"This is only routine procedure," the lawman replied.

"He was right here at home both times, Marshal," spoke up Carmen. "But why do you ask about last night?"

"Because Dave was murdered at that time!" blurted the blacksmith.

The marshal cautioned Abe at the same time that Manuel gasped, "Dave! Marshal, I swear to you, I know nothing of this. How did it happen?"

Bryce told the Lucero family of Dave's being hanged, and he thought it very clear from Manuel's face that the Mexican knew nothing about it. The lawman then stood up and advised, "We'll be going now. Manuel, I must ask you to remain available."

As the two men walked toward the door, Manuel called, "I swear I was here with my family both times, Marshal. On my mother's grave."

Bryce halted and looked back over his shoulder. "I believe you."

Leaving the Luceros, the two men mounted and returned to Juan Gomez's place. There was still no sign of Juan, so they rode back into town to question Dexter Finn.

At the Lucky Dog Saloon the beefy saloonkeeper was sitting at the desk in his small office when the two men came in. His face turned beet-red when the questions were put to him, and sweat broke out on his bald head. Slamming the desk with a meaty fist, Finn bellowed, "I resent this, Bryce! It sounds to me like you think I've been doin' this killin'!"

"*Somebody's* doing it," the marshal retorted. "It's my job to find out who."

"Why come to me?" Finn's eyes were hot.

"Everybody knows you had a grudge against my brother!" blared Abe. "That's why!"

The expression on the saloonkeeper's face changed from anger to fear. "Hey, now wait a minute!" he yelled. "You ain't pinnin' no murders on me! I'll admit I carried a grudge toward Dan, but that was between him and me. It sure ain't nothin' I'd kill him over—and I sure wouldn't kill off any of his kin!"

"I understand you made some pretty sharp remarks to Dan not long before he was killed," said Bryce.

"Well, I was mad," Finn said defensively. "But I didn't put those bullets in his back. The jury's already proven that. Tony Lucero did it. He hanged for it, didn't he?"

"Juries have been wrong before," Bryce countered drily. "And Tony sure didn't kill Bob and his family, nor did he kill Dave. Now, how about telling me where you were Sunday afternoon and last night at suppertime?"

Clearing his throat nervously, Finn declared, "I . . . I was at home."

"Your family was with you, I assume," said Bryce.

"He's a bachelor, Ben," put in Abe. "He lives alone."

Finn scrubbed a shaky hand across his mouth as Bryce asked, "Can anyone verify that you were home? Neighbors, maybe?"

Dexter Finn shook his head. "Nope. I was home alone, and I didn't see anybody either of those times you're askin' about. But I swear to you, Marshal, I ain't killed no one. And just 'cause I can't prove where I was don't make me guilty."

"You're right, it doesn't," agreed Bryce, standing up. "But don't take any trips out of town without talking to me first. Got it?"

"Yeah," replied Finn, his voice husky with resentment. "I got it."

As the two men left the office, the blacksmith scowled at the saloonkeeper, then slammed the office door behind him.

As they walked along the boardwalk toward the marshal's office, Abe mused, "Ben, it just might be him. Did you notice how much he began to sweat the minute you asked where he was those two times?"

"Could be he's our man," Bryce replied, "but on the other hand, he might have started sweating simply because he knew the answer he was going to give me would make him *look* guilty. Anyway, we've got another man to question. I'll go out there around suppertime. Maybe Juan will be home then."

"I'm going with you," insisted Abe.

"All right. I'll drop by your shop when I'm ready to go—but you've got to keep a check on that temper."

"Okay, okay," the big man promised. After a moment or two he remarked, "You know, I just had a thought. Since it looks like the murderer is only going after the Washburn men, maybe he's through killing. Dan, Bob, and Dave are all dead."

"You might be right, Abe," observed Bryce, "except for one small detail."

"What's that?"

"You!" replied the marshal. "You're a male Washburn—and you could be next on the killer's list."

Abe sighed. "I will admit the possibility crossed my mind a time or two, but I haven't been too concerned about being a target. I was thinking that maybe the killer's grudge was toward Dan, so his sons were included for the very reason that they are—*were*—his sons."

"Maybe. But you'd best watch yourself," commented the marshal. "Keep your eyes peeled and look over your shoulder every once in a while. Be careful about being alone, too. As a matter of fact, maybe I ought to stay with you at night till the killer's caught. He no doubt knows you live alone, and my being there just might save your life."

The blacksmith scratched the side of his head, then nodded. "You've got a point there, Ben. You can stay in the spare bedroom. I think I *will* sleep more soundly with you in the house."

Chapter Twelve

After eating a late lunch, Marshal Ben Bryce returned to his office, and he now sat at his desk pondering the situation. Concerned about Abe Washburn, the lawman thought that if the killer's pattern held true, the blacksmith was bound to be the next victim. He was the only male Washburn left.

Bryce thought of Abe's vulnerability even as he worked in his shop. The killer had to be someone everybody in Raton knew, and knew well. The town was too small for someone to live there and remain a stranger. Whoever he was, the man could walk into the blacksmith shop and Abe would never suspect him . . . unless it was Dexter Finn or Juan Gomez. Bryce hoped that Abe had ruled out Manuel Lucero in his mind as a possible suspect.

But if the killer was someone other than those two men, he could go into the shop, pretending to do business, and at the right moment kill Abe with a knife or a blunt instrument. Abe had no doubt escaped assault so far because of his size, marking all the other Washburn men first. Anyone would find the prospect of taking on the muscular giant a daunting one—even a crazed killer. But presuming that the killer was determined to eliminate the last Washburn male and would choose Abe's shop as the place to do so, after completing the deed he could return to the street and no one would be the wiser—that is, until someone found the body. The elusive murderer would have struck again without being caught.

But what then? With his vindictive assault finished, would he continue to live undetected and unpunished, acting and living like any other citizen? Clenching his fists, Ben Bryce vowed to stop him. Surely the man would eventually make a mistake and tip his hand. Bryce hoped the killer's mistake would come before someone else had to die—that someone undoubtedly being Abe Washburn.

Bryce decided to look in on the blacksmith. After donning his coat and hat, he left the office and made his way down the street to Abe's shop. As he approached the big door he heard the wheeze of the bellows and the clang of metal against metal. Pulling the door open, he stepped inside and looked into the interior of the shop. The huge man was beating a red-hot length of scrap iron at the anvil—but a slender youth was working the bellows with a foot while holding another length of iron in the fire. Surprised to see that Abe had an assistant, the lawman recognized the teenager but did not know his name.

Abe looked up as the marshal entered and checked the swing of his hammer. "Hey, Ben," he called, looking bewildered. "Is it quitting time already? You must put in a short day."

Bryce grinned and replied, "No, I was a bit concerned about you being here in the shop alone. Just thought I'd make sure you were all right."

Abe Washburn's ugly face broke into a smile—the first one Ben Bryce had seen in quite a while. "Well, now aren't you just the perfect nursemaid!" he quipped.

The federal man chuckled, then asked, "Who's your helper?"

"He's Charlie Smith's boy," Abe answered, giving the hot iron a hard blow. "Name's Charlie, Junior. He's been wanting to do some work, and with all that's been going on, I've gotten quite a bit behind. And"—he grinned sheepishly—"and I sort of wanted somebody around for the same reason you're here right now. It doesn't hurt to have somebody watching your back."

Bryce nodded, and the youth smiled.

Abe hammered the iron again, then paused and asked, "Say, Ben, how's the wound in your side?"

"Just fine," came the reply.

"Can you do any lifting?"

"Yeah. I'm as good as new now. Why?"

"Soon as I finish with this piece of iron, I can use a hand lifting that old anvil over there into the back of the wagon. I sold it to a rancher east of town when I replaced it with this new one, and I'd like to haul it out to him in a little while. I don't think Charlie's quite strong enough to help me. Just let me finish shaping this iron while it's still hot, and then you can help me hoist the anvil into the bed, okay?"

"Sure," replied the marshal. Grinning, he walked toward the old anvil that rested on a bench.

While Abe pounded the iron again, absorbed in his work, the marshal stepped up to the scarred and battered old anvil. He positioned its protruding ends into the crooks of his elbows and took a deep breath. Lifting the anvil off the bench, he steadied his legs, then turned and carried it to the wagon.

Abe looked up just as Bryce set down the huge hunk of iron in the back of the buckboard. The blacksmith's eyes bulged and his mouth flew open. Laughing and lustily swearing, Abe then exclaimed, "Hey, don't you know that thing weighs almost three hundred pounds?"

Bryce dusted off his hands and replied slyly, "Heck, I used to walk around carrying one of those under each arm. But to be honest, now that I've gotten older, I'm not sure I could still do it."

Abe guffawed and said, "Just remind me never to tangle with you, okay?"

The two men laughed heartily, and Ben Bryce thought how good it felt to laugh. There had been nothing to laugh about in Raton for far too long.

Telling Abe he would see him later, the marshal left the shop and started back to his office. He neared it just in time to see a middle-aged man dash up to his door and pound on it. Breaking into a run, Bryce hollered, "Here I am, mister!"

The man turned and ran toward Bryce, meeting him halfway. Out of breath, the man gasped, "Marshal, you better get over to the Lucky Dog! Hurry! Dexter Finn's gonna cut a man's face off!"

Pivoting, Ben Bryce ran across the street. Seconds later, he barged through the door of the Lucky Dog to find Dexter Finn holding a man on the floor with one hand and attempting to drive the jagged end of a broken whiskey bottle into his face with the other. The man was soaked with sweat as he gripped Finn's wrist with both hands, managing to keep the bottle poised two feet away. Both opponents' arms were quivering from the effort of their contest.

Bryce stormed toward the men and rasped, "That's enough, Finn! Let him up!"

Without giving an inch or looking at the lawman, Finn snarled, "Not till he apologizes! If he don't, he gets this bottle in his face!"

Anger seeped through Bryce's body, tensing it. "I said let him up!"

"This ain't your business!" growled Finn. "I don't have to listen to you, lawman!"

"That's where you're wrong," snapped the marshal. His patience gone, he whipped out his gun and smashed it down on Finn's bald head. The saloon owner collapsed on top of his opponent, the broken bottle slipping harmlessly from his fingers. Bryce rolled Finn's unconscious form off the man, helped him up, and said, "I've seen you around town, sir, but I don't know your name."

His breath coming in short, shaky gasps, the man responded, "Roy Dean, Marshal. I work over at the feedstore."

"So what's this all about?" queried Bryce. "What does Finn want you to apologize for?"

Dean looked down at Finn, who still lay motionless, then replied, "He overheard me telling my friends that it wouldn't surprise me if it turned out that Finn was the killer. He sure had it in for Dan Washburn real bad." The man paused to catch his breath and wipe the sweat from his face with a bandanna.

One of his friends added, "When Finn heard what Roy said, he cut loose with a string of cusswords and grabbed that whiskey bottle from the shelf behind him. He busted the bottom off it on the edge of the bar, then leapt right over the bar and came at Roy like a madman. The rest of us would've tried to help, but none of us wanted to get that bottle jammed into *our* face. When Dexter gets mad, he gets plenty violent."

"Yeah," put in another patron, "and he was plenty mad at Dan Washburn. I'd lay a bet that if you'd lock him up, these killings would stop."

Finn began to stir, moaning in pain. His scalp was cut where the gun barrel had connected, and a large purple lump was rising.

Looking over at the patron, the lawman replied, "I couldn't lock him up for very long, friend. If Mr. Dean wants to press charges, I could hold Finn for a few days, but that's all. I certainly can't lock him up just on suspicion of being the killer. There's nothing to go on."

"I suppose you're right," the man concurred.

Finn regained consciousness, and the lawman helped him to a chair. After getting the two combatants to apologize to each other—one for his rash statement and the other for his rash behavior—Bryce left the saloon and went back to his office.

At dusk Ben Bryce and Abe Washburn went once again to Juan Gomez's place, but the laborer had still not returned. Finding the door unlocked, they entered the house and looked around but found nothing that would incriminate the husky Mexican. As they mounted up, the marshal told Abe they should go to Flora Domingo's to talk with Dolores, for perhaps she might know Juan's whereabouts. Abe agreed, and they trotted back to town.

They reached Flora Domingo's house, and she immediately responded to their knock, welcoming the two men with a smile.

"I need to talk to Dolores, Mrs. Domingo," the marshal declared without preamble.

"She is not here," replied the slender Mexican woman. "Dolores is staying with Wilma Washburn. As you know, Señor Abe, Dolores and Wilma are close friends. My niece offered to move in with Wilma for a while, and Wilma gladly accepted. She does not want to be alone."

"That is very kind of Dolores, Mrs. Domingo," Abe responded. "Well, I guess we'll see her at Wilma's then. Thank you."

Mounting their horses yet again, the men rode across town to Wilma Washburn's house. When Wilma ushered them inside, Abe explained to the newly widowed young woman that Marshal Bryce wanted to talk to Dolores. Wilma led them to the kitchen, where Dolores was sitting in her wheelchair at the table, kneading dough.

The beautiful Mexican looked up at the men and smiled warmly. "Good evening, Señor Washburn . . . Marshal Bryce. Did I hear that you wish to talk to me, Marshal?"

Bryce nodded. "I wonder if you know where Juan Gomez might be, Dolores."

"No, I do not," she replied. "You have been to his house?"

"Yes. We just left there. As a matter of fact, we've gone out there three times today."

"Sometimes his jobs keep him away for several days," Dolores advised. "He no doubt is working somewhere out of town." Then a frown creased her brow, and her dark eyes looked troubled. "Why are you looking for Juan?"

"I want to ask him some questions. I want to see if he can establish his whereabouts at the times that Bob and his family and Dave were killed."

Wilma sank onto a chair at the table, studying the marshal's face intently, and Dolores's mouth fell open.

Noting Dolores's shock, Bryce explained, "Juan had plenty of reason to want to get rid of Tony Lucero. I don't have to convince you of that, do I?"

"Well, no, Marshal, but I assure you, Juan is no killer. Besides, I do not understand what Juan's conflict with Tony has to do with these killings."

"I may be barking up the wrong tree altogether, but it might just be that Juan decided to kill Marshal Washburn and let the blame fall on Tony. Not only would it get Tony out of the way, he could then avoid suspicion by using Tony's threat against Dan Washburn. He'd then further avoid suspicion by killing others as well."

"I do not believe it," Dolores retorted heatedly. "I know Juan, and I just cannot believe he is a murderer, Marshal. It cannot be true."

"I hope you're right," Bryce sighed, "but one thing's for sure—we've got a killer on our hands, and Juan remains a suspect until he can establish an alibi."

There was an awkward silence for a few moments, but Abe Washburn ended it by thanking Dolores for staying with Wilma. He and Wilma then briefly discussed Dave's burial, which would be the next morning.

A knock sounded at the door, and Ben Bryce volunteered to answer it. Opening the door, he found John Townsend standing there, his medical bag in hand. The physician had come to check on Wilma, fearing that with all she had been through, she might lose her baby. Bryce led the doctor to the kitchen, then he suggested to Abe that they go see how Darlene and Lisa Washburn were doing. The two men excused themselves and showed themselves out.

They arrived at Darlene's house just as she and Lisa were about to eat supper. Two more places were set, and while they were eating, Bryce filled the women in on his talks with Dexter Finn and Manuel Lucero—and told them that Juan Gomez seemed to have disappeared.

"It could be," noted the marshal, "that he's hiding out and doing these killings."

Darlene reached for her brother-in-law's hand. "Just make sure you take good care of yourself, Abe," she told him with a note of fear in her voice. "You're all Wilma, Lisa, and I have now. We couldn't bear losing you, too."

When the meal was finished, Darlene asked the blacksmith to stay in the kitchen and talk to her about Dave's funeral, giving Ben and Lisa the opportunity to spend a few minutes alone together. The young woman led the marshal to the parlor, and entering the room, Lisa turned to Bryce and looked at him with sorrowful eyes.

"You poor thing," he murmured tenderly.

"Oh, Ben," she declared, embracing him and laying her head on his chest, "I want this horrible nightmare to be over."

"It will be," he assured her, holding her tight. "That murdering devil is going to make a mistake one of these days, and then I'll have him."

Lisa shuddered. "I pray that day will come soon."

Bryce held the beautiful blonde tight, delighting in her sweet smell. He bent his head and kissed her—tentatively at first, then passionately. Then he abruptly pulled away, muttering, "Forgive me, Lisa. I had no right. . . ."

"Of course you did. I wanted you to."

"But here you are, in the midst of all this tragedy. It's unfair of me to add to everything you're dealing with right now."

She pulled away from him and stared deeply into his eyes. "Ben Bryce, you are the one thing in my life that is keeping me from falling apart. I promise you, you are *not* making things more difficult for me. Quite the contrary."

Standing on her tiptoes, she lifted her lips to his, and they kissed again. They stood embracing for a few moments longer until they heard Abe and Darlene coming down the hallway from the kitchen. They abruptly released each other and waited side by side.

The two men stayed for a few more minutes, then left, heading for Abe's house.

Although it was at least an hour past midnight, sleep eluded Dolores Domingo. She lay awake in her room at Wilma Washburn's house, worrying about Juan Gomez and wondering where he might be. Suddenly she heard a strange sound, a muffled thumping noise, and it seemed to come from somewhere in the house. The sound was repeated, and this time she was sure it had come from Wilma's room, right next door.

Dolores pulled herself to a sitting position and, leaning toward the bedstand, struck a match and lit the lamp. Struggling with her lifeless legs, she draped them over the side of the bed and, with difficulty, worked her way into her wheelchair.

Holding the lamp in her lap, Dolores wheeled herself to the bedroom door, opened it, and moved quickly down the hall to Wilma's room. She turned the knob and shoved the door open, spilling lamplight into the room. Dolores was shocked to see a man standing over Wilma's bed—and a large knife protruding from the center of Wilma's chest.

Recognizing the man, Dolores gasped, "Oh, my God! It's you! I can't believe it! Oh, no! *No* . . ."

The killer went for Dolores, and her bloodcurdling screams filled the room. "Shut up!" he growled. "Shut up!" Grabbing a heavy candle holder that stood on the dresser, he smashed it savagely on her head. The impact tipped the wheelchair over, and Dolores tumbled to the floor. The lamp on her lap crashed, sending kerosene and flames in every direction. The killer was about to make sure Dolores was dead when he heard male voices outside calling to each other and coming on the run.

Swearing vehemently, the man wheeled and quickly jumped out the bedroom window through which he had entered. Just as his feet hit the ground, he heard the front door crash in. Without a moment's hesitation he sprinted away from the house to safety.

Ethel Mitchell ran across the yard, pulling on a robe, as her husband and son broke open the front door of Wilma Washburn's house. Ethel smelled the smoke and dashed down the hallway to Wilma's bedroom, finding the two men trying to beat out the fire with blankets. She cried out in horror at the sight of Wilma's pregnant body lying with the knife in her chest. Sickened, she looked away and saw the overturned wheelchair and Dolores's unconscious form lying next to it.

While the men extinguished the flames, Ethel took hold of Dolores's arms and dragged her into the hall. Her husband and son came out of the bedroom just as Ethel lit a lamp and knelt to examine Dolores.

"Wilma's dead, Ethel," her husband groaned. "Is Dolores—?"

"She's alive, Gary," Ethel replied, holding fingertips to the side of the invalid's neck. She turned to her son and ordered, "Wayne, run and get Doc Townsend. Quick!"

The teenager was about to bolt when his father suggested, "It might be best to just carry her to the clinic. Wayne, you run ahead and wake Doc up so he'll be expecting us. I'll put Dolores in her chair and wheel her over. As soon as she's in Doc's hands, we'll go to the hotel—I understand that's where the marshal's living now—and tell Bryce what's happened."

At Abe Washburn's house Marshal Ben Bryce was sleeping fully clothed in the spare bedroom, where he had left a low-burning lamp on the small table beside the bed. Exhausted from the events of the past twenty-four hours, the federal marshal slept soundly. But suddenly Bryce was startled awake by the blast of two gunshots, followed by shattering glass. Grabbing the lamp, he flew out of his bedroom, running toward Abe's room with the lamp in one hand and his cocked revolver in the other. As he dashed down the hallway he heard three more rapid shots. Kicking open Abe's door and ready to fire, he saw the big man standing at the shattered window with a smoking gun in his hand. Blood was spreading down the upper left sleeve of his long johns.

"What happened?" asked Bryce, moving close.

Breathing hard, the big blacksmith gasped, "I wasn't sleeping too well, just dozing some, when I heard a noise outside the window. I immediately started to roll out of bed when two shots came through the glass. One of 'em got me. I grabbed my gun off the bedstand and sent three shots after him, but I don't think I hit him."

"Did you get a look at him?" asked Bryce.

"Naw. All I saw was a dark figure. Couldn't tell anything about his size or his height. He was gone too quick." Shaking his head, he added, "Guess I should've put curtains on my windows. I sure made it easy for the killer to figure out which room I sleep in."

Helping the big man to a chair, Ben advised, "Get a good hold on your arm and try to stay the flow of blood. I'll go get Dr. Townsend. Is the slug in your arm?"

Abe felt the wound. "I don't think so. Feels like it went on through."

"Think you'll be all right till I come back with Doc?"

"Sure. Go ahead."

Bryce turned, then paused at the bed. Leaning down, holding the lamp up, he found two holes in the bedding where the bullets had plowed into the mattress. The lawman whistled and shook his head. "Boy, that was close, Abe. Good thing you *weren't* sleeping too soundly, or he'd have killed you."

Bryce was about to leave when he heard excited voices in the yard, followed by a knock at the front door. Hurrying to answer the summons, he found two of Abe's neighbors standing there, guns in their hands. Just behind them, Gary and Wayne Mitchell were coming on the run.

"Marshal, we heard shots!" one of Abe's neighbors declared. "It sounded like they came from Abe's house."

"They did," confirmed Bryce. "Our killer just tried to do away with Abe. Shot him in the arm, but he's okay."

Wayne Mitchell jumped onto the porch, out of breath. "Marshal!" the young man gasped. "The hotel clerk told us you were staying with Abe. Wilma Washburn was stabbed to death a few minutes ago. The killer broke into the house, put a knife in her chest, and clubbed poor Dolores Domingo. She's still alive, but she's hurt bad. We took her to Doc Townsend's, but he said it doesn't look good. She's unconscious."

Punching his fist into his palm, Ben Bryce swore under his breath. "That dirty devil!" he said aloud. "He must have done his bloody work on Wilma, then hurried over here to kill Abe." Rubbing the back of his neck, he mumbled, "The man's a maniac. He's not only after the Washburn men, he's—" He stopped in midsentence.

"What's the matter, Marshal?" Wayne Mitchell asked, seeing Bryce's eyes widen.

"He's after the Washburn women, too!" exclaimed the lawman, bolting through the door. He called over his shoulder as he ran, "Lisa and Darlene are in danger! Take Abe to the doctor's, will you?"

There were no lights showing in any of the windows of Darlene's house as Ben Bryce rounded the corner and sprinted toward it. Running flat out the last few yards, Bryce felt his stomach tie into knots. What if the killer had started at Darlene's house first, wanting to finish his gruesome task all in one night? *Please, God, no!* he prayed. *Not Lisa!*

The lawman's heart banged against his rib cage as he leapt onto the porch and began pounding on the door. Beating on the door incessantly, he asked himself why the killer would want to kill the women. Then he realized he already had the answer: The man was a maniac, and the killings did not have to make sense. Or maybe in his demented mind he believed his mission in life was to wipe out the entire Washburn family.

Bryce continued pounding, peering through the window just beside the door, and finally he saw a flare of light from a lamp being lit. Breathing a prayer of thanks, he waited impatiently on the front porch. Presently he heard Lisa's voice call, "Who is it?"

"Ben!" he responded loudly. "It's Ben!"

The lock rattled and the door came open. Holding the lamp high, the lovely blonde stepped back so the lawman could enter. Her eyes were filled with sleep, and her voice was husky as she asked, "What is it? What's wrong?"

"Have you heard or seen anything out of the ordinary?" he asked in turn.

"No," Lisa replied, closing the door behind him. "I was sound asleep when you knocked. I haven't heard or seen anything."

"Thank God!" Bryce breathed, folding her into his arms.

"Ben, what is it? What's happened?"

Releasing her, the marshal told her gently, "You'd better sit down, honey. The killer's been at it again."

"Oh, no!" she choked. "Don't tell me he murdered Uncle Abe!"

Taking the lamp from her, Bryce guided Lisa to a chair in the parlor, then set the lamp on a table. He knelt in front of her, taking her hands in his. "The man shot at Abe through his bedroom window, honey, but he's all right. He was alerted by a sound outside the window just in time to dodge two bullets that would have killed him had he been sleeping. Fortunately he only sustained a superficial wound. *Unfortunately,* the killer got away." Sighing, Bryce added, "The real bad news is that before he went after Abe, he broke into Wilma's house. He . . . he stabbed Wilma in the chest. She's dead."

Lisa was horror-struck. "Oh, no!" she whispered as tears filled her eyes. "The baby . . . " Her body began trembling. Shaking her head in disbelief, she asked, "What about Dolores?" The federal man told her all that he knew, adding, "I'm going over to the clinic as soon as I leave here."

Lisa suddenly broke into heavy sobs, murmuring Wilma's name over and over. Ben Bryce put his arms around her and held her tight until her weeping subsided. Pulling away from him slightly, she mumbled, "I have to tell Mother."

Bryce suggested, "She's obviously so exhausted that even my pounding didn't arouse her, so let's let her sleep, Lisa. She's suffered so many losses, there's no reason to wake her to tell her more terrible news. It can keep till morning."

"You're right," the young woman responded, sniffing. "Morning will be soon enough. I want to look in on her, though, and make sure she's resting all right."

"Sure," Bryce agreed, rising to his feet. He watched while Lisa lit a second lamp and carried it down the hall toward Darlene's room. As he waited in the parlor, his heart went out to Lisa. She had experienced so much grief in the past few days. Thank God, she still had her mother and her uncle Abe.

The marshal kept his eyes on Lisa until she disappeared from his sight around the corner of the hall. Suddenly a chilling scream pierced the air, echoing through the house, and the lawman raced down the hall and into Darlene's room. Lisa stood rooted in horror, holding the lamp and screaming repeatedly.

Bryce gasped as he saw Darlene's lifeless body sprawled crosswise on the bed, lying on her back. Her head and arms dangled over the edge of the bed, and her sightless eyes bulged from their sockets.

The lawman took the lamp from Lisa Washburn's hand and placed it on the nightstand. When her terror-filled eyes focused on his face, she stopped screaming and her knees buckled. Bryce gathered her into his arms and carried her into her own room, laying her on the bed. Crossing the room to the dresser, he lit the lamp, then sat down beside her. He took her hands in his and whispered, "I'm so sorry, my darling."

Lisa pulled her hands loose and wrapped her arms around his neck, holding on to him as if her life depended on it. Then she began sobbing uncontrollably, deep wracking sobs that tore at Ben Bryce's heart.

After a while Lisa's crying ebbed, and Bryce took out his handkerchief, handing it to her. She dabbed at her swollen eyes, blew her nose, and murmured shakily, "Oh, Ben! What am I going to do? Dear God, what am I going to do?"

He held her tightly, promising, "Don't worry. I'll make sure you'll be all right."

The young woman was silent for a few moments, then she said angrily, "The man who's done this, he's got to be completely insane. Like some rabid animal. There can't be any other explanation."

"I agree, honey," replied the marshal. "I'm just so thankful he didn't get his hands on you, too."

Lisa suddenly stared at the marshal. Trembling fingertips went to her lips. "Ben, why didn't he?"

"Why didn't he what?"

"Why didn't he get his hands on me? He's killed everyone else in my family except Uncle Abe—and he tried to kill *him*. I was right here in this house when he . . . when he killed Mother. Whoever he is, he had to have known that. Why didn't he kill me?"

"There's no way to know that until we catch him," Ben Bryce commented softly. He then stood up and told her, "I need to go look in your mother's room. The killer might have left some kind of clue."

Fear touched Lisa's dark blue eyes. "Please don't leave me, Ben! Don't leave me alone! Let me come with you!"

"Are you sure you should? At least let me go cover your mother's body first."

"No," insisted Lisa firmly, shaking her head. "I . . . I want to look at her."

"Are you sure?"

"Yes. Let's go."

Lisa's body shook violently when they returned to Darlene's room. She closed her eyes and clung to Bryce for a few seconds, then moved to the bed and stood over her mother's body. The lawman knelt down, and noting the mottled discoloration around Darlene's mouth and the purple marks on her throat, he concluded that she had been strangled to death. Darlene's bulging eyes and contorted mouth told of the terror in her final moments of life, and the way the pillows were strewn and the covers were rumpled showed that she had struggled hard against her attacker.

While Lisa looked on, frozen in silence, the federal man composed Darlene's body, then covered her completely with a blanket. Taking the lamp from the nightstand, he carried it to the window. It was open, the cold night air toying with the curtains—mute testimony to the killer's means of entry and escape.

Closing the window, Bryce then looked carefully around the room, but the killer had left nothing behind that might give a clue as to his identity. Turning to the harried young woman, he said, "Lisa, I'm going to see to it that you aren't alone for a single minute until that madman is caught. For now, come to Dr. Townsend's office with me. Dolores Domingo just might have seen the killer's face—and if she's awake, and she did, I'll know whom to arrest."

"Okay," Lisa mumbled, brushing a stray lock of blond hair from her eyes and glancing briefly at the blanket-covered form on the bed. "It'll just take me a minute to get dressed, and then we can go."

Chapter Thirteen

It was just past three o'clock in the morning when Ben Bryce and Lisa Washburn walked into John Townsend's office. They found Dr. Townsend standing over Abe Washburn, who lay on the examining table with his left arm heavily bandaged. On the other side of the room, on a bed beside the wall, Dolores Domingo lay unconscious.

The lawman immediately told Abe about Darlene's murder, and Lisa left Bryce's side and rushed to her uncle. Burying her face close to his neck, she sobbed, "Oh, Uncle Abe! We're the only ones left!"

The big man curled his good arm around her, telling her soothingly, "Don't you worry about a thing, honey. From now till that killer is caught, I'm not gonna let you out of my sight. And when this horrible thing is over, Uncle Abe will take care of you. Everything will be all right. I promise."

Reassured that Lisa would be safe with her giant of an uncle, Bryce asked Townsend, "Any permanent damage to Abe's arm?"

"Nope," replied the physician with a slight smile. "Aside from being mighty lucky that he wasn't killed, the bullet also missed the bone. Good thing, too. Otherwise his blacksmithing days might have been over."

Looking across the room to Dolores Domingo, Bryce offered, "Doc, since she was found in Wilma's room, there's a good chance Dolores might have seen the killer's face before he hit her. When she wakes up, she can tell us who it was."

"That may well be true, but I think you'll have to solve this case without her help. You see, she's in a coma, Ben. It may be a long time before she wakes up . . . if she ever does."

Bryce's head whipped around. "Oh, no! It's that bad?"

"He hit her plenty hard," replied Townsend. "Mighty near caved in her skull. All we can do now is hope . . . and pray."

The next morning, after eating a meager breakfast, Ben Bryce and Lisa Washburn mounted horses and trotted across town. While assisting Abe Washburn back to his house a few hours earlier, it was arranged that Lisa would stay with him at night until the killer was caught. Neither Abe nor Bryce would allow her to be alone for a minute. Meanwhile, the young woman wanted to accompany the lawman when he went to question Manuel Lucero and Dexter Finn as to their whereabouts the night before.

As they rode toward the saloonkeeper's house, the marshal asked, "Are you sure it wouldn't be better if you stayed with your uncle today?"

"I'll be there tonight," she replied. "I'd rather be with you now—if that's okay."

He smiled lovingly. "Of course it's okay. It's *more* than okay. But I'm concerned that going with me to question these suspects will be too much for you to bear."

Shaking her head, Lisa insisted, "All I feel right now is numb. The reality of what's happened hasn't sunk in yet." She sighed, adding softly, "Although I know it will before too long."

Reaching Finn's house, the lawman knocked on the front door and waited for a response. An elderly woman opened the door. Querying her, Bryce learned that she lived down the street from Finn and had been in his house to care for him. The blow to the head that the saloon owner had sustained left him dizzy, and he was having spells of nausea. The silver-haired woman, whom Lisa knew well, attested that Dexter Finn had not left the house all night.

That information removed Finn as a suspect—which did not really surprise the marshal. Although the saloon-keeper was obviously hot-tempered, he had not struck the lawman as a crazed killer who would murder innocent women and children to get revenge on Dan Washburn.

Bryce and Lisa mounted up and headed to Manuel Lucero's place. The marshal hated to bother Manuel again, but since some people might still think of him as a possible suspect, it was Bryce's duty to follow proper procedure and make the Mexican prove he had been home all during the night.

Manuel was obviously shocked and saddened to learn of the latest deaths. When the marshal asked him where he had been the night before—assuring him that it was merely a routine question—Manuel swore he had not left the house after supper, and his wife and daughters backed him up. After the Luceros extended their sympathy to Lisa, the lawman and the young woman headed back toward town.

As they rode, he remarked, "I feel strongly that it's Juan Gomez. It's *got* to be him. He's lurking somewhere around town, and I've got to find him before he tries to kill Abe again—and comes after you."

Lisa was silent for a time, then she turned to Bryce and there was puzzlement in her eyes as she looked at him and said, "I just can't figure it, Ben. What on earth could Juan have against the Washburn family? And if it's all of us he wants to kill, why didn't he kill me last night as well as . . . as well as Mother?"

"It doesn't make any sense," the lawman replied,

"but making sense is something that a rational mind does. Juan may have been rational when he shot your dad in the back to frame Tony, but maybe his mind snapped at that point. Maybe he's simply an insane man killing Washburns for no reason. The first murder might have unleashed a psychopathic killer."

Lisa merely shook her head sadly.

When they arrived back in town, Bryce suggested, "Look, I've got to search for Juan's hiding place, and you're totally exhausted. Let me take you to your uncle's house so you can rest."

So tired that she could barely sit her horse any longer, Lisa readily agreed.

Arriving at Abe's house, they knocked, and after a moment the big man opened the door, holding his Colt .45 in his right hand. He let them in, saying, "I've got some coffee just finished brewing. Come on in and sit down."

They followed him into the kitchen. As Lisa went to the cupboard and took down two cups, Abe adjusted the sling that held his left arm and asked, "How goes the investigation?"

Bryce explained that both Dexter Finn and Manuel Lucero had solid alibis. They were no longer suspects.

"So we're down to Juan, eh?" Abe asked.

"Yep."

"Any sign of him?"

"None," replied the marshal. "I'm leaving Lisa in your care while I turn this town upside down. Juan's hiding someplace, and I'm going to flush him out."

Abe patted the revolver where it lay on the table next to his cup, a wry grin on his ugly face. "Don't you worry, Marshal. I'll take care of Lisa."

Ben Bryce finished his coffee, then rose and stated, "I'll stop by periodically while I'm playing bloodhound. See that Lisa rests, will you, Abe?"

"You can bet on it," the blacksmith assured him.

Bryce suddenly asked, "Is that arm hurting you?

Maybe I should get someone to come and stay with the two of you. I mean, if Juan should try to bust in here and that arm is giving you trouble, you might not be able to—"

"Don't you worry, Ben," cut in Abe. "A little pain won't keep me down. I can handle anything Juan can throw at us. Lisa is perfectly safe. You just go track down that killer. I guarantee you, if he shows up here, he's a dead man."

The handsome marshal leaned down and kissed Lisa on the cheek. "You try and get some sleep, young lady. I'll check on you later."

Lisa nodded as she looked at him lovingly. "All right."

"You're not afraid, are you?"

"Not with my big strong uncle to protect me," she replied, smiling affectionately at Abe.

Bryce left, and Abe bolted the door behind him. He then went around the house checking the locks on the windows, and Lisa followed him like a frightened puppy. When they had completed their inspection and returned to the kitchen, she looked up at the giant of a man with tears in her eyes. "Oh, Uncle Abe, we're the only Washburns left! Ben has got to find Juan and stop him!"

Abe took Lisa into his good arm and held her tight. "It's gonna be all right, honey. This whole thing will be over soon. Now, you see if you can get some sleep—and don't worry. Your Uncle Abe will never let anything happen to you."

Marshal Ben Bryce began an extensive search. Working fast, he inspected every house, barn, and shed in and around Raton. Twice during the day he looked in at Abe's house, finding all was well and Lisa asleep. Returning to John Townsend's clinic, he stopped in, but there was still no change in Dolores Domingo's condition.

As darkness began settling over Raton, Ben Bryce felt

angry and frustrated. The suspect was not to be found. He decided to ride out to Juan Gomez's house one more time, hoping that he had overlooked a clue as to where the laborer was hiding.

Dr. John Townsend was sterilizing some instruments when he heard a low moan. Wheeling around, he saw Dolores Domingo stirring, showing signs of waking.

Dashing across the room, Townsend began to bathe the lovely young woman's face with cool water. She moaned again and her eyes began to flutter. The doctor's heart quickened, and a smile wreathing his weathered face, he encouraged, "Atta girl! Come on! Wake up!"

It took several more minutes for Dolores's eyes to fully open. Happy to know she was going to be all right, Townsend bent close and asked softly, "Dolores, do you recognize me?"

The young woman ran her tongue over her lips in an attempt to reply. The physician fetched a cup of water and lifted her head slightly, letting her drink a few drops at a time. When she had taken a sufficient amount, he asked again, "Do you know me, Dolores?"

Nodding slowly, she replied weakly, "*Sí.* Doctor Townsend."

The physician was elated. "That's right!" Then his face sobered. "You were at Wilma's house. Do you remember what happened?"

Dolores suddenly looked terrified.

"You *do* remember, don't you?"

Tears filled Dolores's dark eyes. "Oh, Doctor, it was terrible! He murdered Wilma! I saw the knife in her body! Then he . . . he came at me!"

"Dolores," urged Townsend, "who was it? Who came at you and tried to kill you?"

Her lips quivering, the young woman began to whimper. She closed her eyes as if trying to shut out the horrifying image.

"Come on, girl!" breathed Townsend. "Tell me! Who was it?"

"I cannot believe it!" she sobbed. "I cannot believe it!" She began weeping and mumbling incoherently.

"Dolores, please!" pressed the physician. "Calm down and talk to me. This is very, very important."

But the young woman continued to weep. Aware that he would get no further until Dolores was able to compose herself, Townsend stood patiently beside her bed. It was just a matter of moments before they would finally learn the identity of the man who had systematically killed off almost the entire Washburn family.

It was completely dark outside as late afternoon turned into evening, and Lisa Washburn nervously paced the kitchen floor in front of the stove. Preparing a meal for her uncle, who sat at the kitchen table sipping a cup of coffee, the young woman was waiting for a pot of water to boil before putting in the potatoes, and it seemed to be taking forever.

Abe watched his beautiful niece and laughed. "You're gonna wear a rut in the floor, girl. Don't worry. No one can get in here, honey. The doors are bolted and the windows are locked." He patted the revolver lying beside his right hand, adding, "And even if someone did get in, this'd stop him fast."

"That's not what I'm worried about, Uncle Abe," Lisa replied. "It's been nearly four hours since Ben was here last. Maybe something has gone wrong. Maybe he found Juan and— Oh, Uncle Abe, if something's happened to Ben, I couldn't stand it! I just could not stand it!"

The huge blacksmith rose to his feet and laid a hand gently on her shoulder. "Don't worry about that young lawman. He can take care of himself. You've been through too much lately, Lisa," he told her tenderly. "Your nerves are about to let go. Now, you just get a good hold on yourself. Everything's gonna be okay."

Lisa managed a smile and rested her head against her

uncle's massive chest. He fitted her snugly into his powerful right arm and pressed her body closer to his. "Thank you for giving me strength," she told him.

"I love you, Lisa," he whispered. "I'd do anything for you." He squeezed her tighter, and Lisa felt as though she were being crushed. She lifted her head to tell him that he was hurting her, and without warning he planted a passionate kiss on her lips.

Lisa was shocked and attempted to squirm from his powerful grasp, but he held her fast. He finally broke off the kiss, and she gasped, "Uncle Abe! Are you mad?"

For an answer, he forced his thick lips on hers again, kissing her long and hard.

Lisa tried to scream, but the only sound that came out was a stifled whine. Then he pulled his head back, and she shouted, "Uncle Abe! Let go of me!"

"I'll never let go of you, my precious beauty," he vowed, his voice husky with longing. "I'm in love with you, Lisa. I have been ever since you became a mature woman."

Lisa Washburn could not believe what was happening. Pushing against him, she shrieked, "Let me go! Do you hear me? I said, let me go!"

Not giving an inch, the huge man said, "I want you to marry me, Lisa. We'll be very happy together."

"Uncle Abe! Have you lost your mind?"

"Listen to me," he directed, looking at her hungrily. "I love you. Don't you understand? And if you promise to marry me, I'll let you live and you'll be rich—very rich. We'll be happy together. Happier than you could ever dream!"

"You're hurting me!" Lisa blurted. "Let go! I am *not* going to marry you! This is insane! *You* are insane!"

The huge man seemed stung by her words, and his eyes suddenly turned dangerous. His arm pressed her tighter against his body as he repeated urgently, "If you promise to marry me, we'll be rich."

Disgusted and terrified, Lisa looked up at him aghast.

"What . . . what do you mean, we'll be rich?" she stammered.

Abe smiled at her. "Ah! I see I have your interest. That's better. After I show you, we'll talk about getting married."

"Show me what?" she asked, pushing against him.

Abe grabbed her by the wrist. "Come with me," he insisted, dragging her into his parlor.

Lisa had to scurry not to stumble. Trying to keep her mind clear, she wondered how she would be able to get away from him. How could she flee the house? He would surely stop her before she had time to unbolt a door or unlock a window. She would never be able to get out unless somehow Abe was incapacitated, and there was no way on earth she could manage to overpower him.

Crossing the room, Abe pulled a desk drawer open and extracted an envelope. Thrusting it into her hand, he grunted, "Read this."

Lisa read the return address. It was from an attorney in St. Louis, Missouri, and was addressed to Daniel H. Washburn—her father. Eyeing Abe warily, she asked, "How did you get my father's mail?"

Abe laughed evilly, reminding her, "You know I was always the one who picked up the mail from the stage office and brought Dan what was his. I was your daddy's messenger boy, didn't you know?" There was bitterness in his voice. "I was always real conscientious, too—except for this letter. This one got my curiosity up, so I kept it without Dan's knowing about it. Sure glad I did. Go on, read it."

Lisa's hands trembled as she removed the letter and began to read. In the first line was a name she had known all of her life—Matilda Harrington, a wealthy aunt of Dan and Abe's. Lisa had met her great-aunt Matilda only once, when she was a small child. As she recalled, the woman had married a very wealthy man.

The other thing she recalled was that Aunt Matilda had never liked Abe.

Reading on, Lisa learned that Matilda Harrington had recently died, leaving $400,000 to Dan—and nothing to Abe. The attorney explained that the will stipulated if Dan was deceased at the time the fortune was to be given him, it was to go to his wife. If Darlene should also be deceased, the money was to be divided equally among Dan's children and their spouses and descendants. In the event that neither Dan nor any of his family were alive, the money would be given to charity. The money was due to be issued on October 31, 1887 . . . tomorrow.

Suddenly Lisa's blood turned to ice—Abe Washburn was the killer! She had been spared because one of Dan's descendants had to be alive to receive the money, and apparently Abe's twisted mind reasoned that he could frighten her into marriage by threatening her life.

Nausea clawed at Lisa's stomach, and her pulse pounded in her temples. Her voice catching, she asked, "How . . . how could you have done such terrible deeds? How could you have murdered your own family?"

Abe stared intensely into her frightened eyes. "I always wanted to be rich, and I figured this was the only chance I'd ever get."

Hatred toward her uncle welled up inside Lisa Washburn. She tried to speak, but her throat tightened, choking off the words.

The blacksmith snatched the envelope from her hand and tossed it on the desk. Pressing his body against Lisa's, he grinned lasciviously. "Hey, girl, I let you live! The money is yours! We can get married and live happily for the rest of our lives! Like I said, I always wanted you anyway . . . only now you're even more desirable." Then his face hardened, and he demanded, "Well? Are you gonna marry me? Don't forget, I only have to keep you alive for another twenty-four hours and the money's all mine, with you or without you—although I'd sure rather it be with you. See, all I have to do is keep you tied up and gagged till then. When Ben comes around to find out how you are, I'll just keep telling him you're sleeping, completely exhausted from all that's happened."

He picked up another paper from the desk and waved it in front of Lisa's face. "You gotta sign this for me, attesting that you're Dan's only living heir. 'Course if you don't, I'll just forge your name—but it'd make things a whole lot easier if you do. For *both* of us."

He paused, then asked, "So what's it gonna be? If you say yes, as soon as I've got hold of the money, we'll leave town in the middle of the night. I'll leave a letter saying we just couldn't bear to stay here where our whole family was murdered, and we had to go away immediately." Looking into her eyes, he remarked, "You'll see, Lisa. Marrying me won't be so bad." Then he laughed wickedly, adding, "But maybe you think it's a fate worse than death. Well, girl, that's your other choice."

She barely heard his words as she stared into his ugly face. Her mind was spinning, and all she could think of was that she wanted to hurt him as much as he had hurt her. Forcing herself to think rationally, she lowered her eyes and found herself looking at his bandaged arm. Finding her voice, she muttered, "How did you get the gunshot wound in your arm?"

Abe laughed, obviously pleased with himself. "I staged the whole thing. I jabbed the end of a rasp through both sides of my arm to make it look like a bullet had gone through it." Narrowing his eyes, he declared, "I thought of everything, honey. The only hitch in the scheme was that stupid Dolores. If she hadn't left her room, I wouldn't have bothered with her. My only worry now is that she might come out of the coma and name me before I can get to her and snuff out her life."

Shaking her head at the unreality of it all, Lisa felt as though she were in a horrid nightmare and could not wake up. She was sickened and terrified and furious all at once. Did he honestly believe that she would marry her own uncle, much less the cold-blooded murderer of her parents, her brothers, and their families? Then another realization struck her. Unable to look at the blacksmith, she asked, "You're also responsible for Tony Lucero's death, aren't you? You let an innocent young man hang for a crime he did not commit."

Laughing, Abe replied, "Oh, yeah. I just happened to be heading home from a poker game when I saw Tony and your dad talking in the street—and I knew I had the perfect chance to kill my first Washburn. It's too bad about Tony being hanged," he mused, "since he wasn't on my list. But I had to frame him. It worked beautifully!"

Her gorge rising, Lisa did not know until that moment how much she could hate. Feeling dizzy, she put her hand on the desk to steady herself. There was no doubt in her mind that her uncle would kill her without blinking if she did not promise to marry him—but she also knew she could never make the words come out of her mouth. Somehow she had to get away from him; somehow— Then she remembered the Colt .45 lying on the kitchen table. If she could only get to it . . .

Chapter Fourteen

Collecting quietly across the road from Abe Washburn's house were Dr. John Townsend and six other armed men he had rounded up. They were about to set into motion a plan to lure the big blacksmith to his door so they could capture him. Townsend prayed the plan would work but felt he had no choice but to try. Marshal Ben Bryce had not been in his office, and the physician did not dare wait a moment longer, knowing Lisa Washburn was with Abe. Suddenly hoofbeats were heard, and Townsend turned his head. He breathed a sigh of relief when he saw that the rider was the marshal. He raised his arm and hailed him, and the lawman directed his horse toward Townsend.

Sliding from the saddle, Bryce looked at the men curiously and asked, "What's going on? Doc, what are you doing here?"

The physician stepped close to the lawman and exclaimed, "Marshal, am I glad to see you!"

"I was out at Juan Gomez's house," the lawman explained. "Juan finally returned—from a job he'd been doing out of town. That established his innocence, so I'm back to square one as far as who the killer is." Shaking his head, he added, "I was so sure it was Juan. But as a matter of fact, the last I saw of him, he was heading for your clinic to see Dolores. If she had regained consciousness, he was going to ask her if she would marry him. I was going to stop in there myself as soon as I'd made sure things were all right here." Puzzled, he asked again, "What's going on?"

"Dolores *did* regain consciousness. Shortly after you left my office," the physician answered. "She saw the killer, all right—and it's Abe Washburn! When I couldn't locate you, I gathered these men to help me capture him."

Ben Bryce's chest went tight. "Abe!" he gasped. "My God! Lisa's in there with him!"

Nodding, Townsend said, "I figured she was. That's why I was in such a hurry."

Thinking fast, Bryce suggested, "Maybe it's best if you men just stay back here in the shadows and let me handle this. Abe isn't aware that Dolores has identified him, and they're expecting me back. I'll just go up to the door and act as though nothing has happened. When Abe lets me in, I'll take him."

"Better be plenty careful. We don't want to get Lisa hurt."

Nodding, Bryce assured him, "Don't worry. I'd sooner lay down my life than let anything happen to that young woman."

Townsend frowned and asked, "You . . . you don't suppose he's . . . harmed her already, do you?"

"I doubt it. He could easily have killed her last night when he strangled Darlene, but he didn't, so for some reason he's spared her. I'm glad I got here when I did. If you men had stormed the place, Lisa might have gotten hurt." Glancing at the men, Bryce commanded, "I'm going in now. You fellas stay out of sight till I holler for you."

Without waiting for a response, Ben Bryce dashed up the walk toward the door. If he got no response to his knock, he would break down the door if necessary.

Inside, Lisa Washburn managed to wrench free of Abe's grip. Quick and agile, the young woman eluded him when he tried to grab her and raced to the kitchen, knowing her only hope was to get her hands on Abe's gun. She ran to the table, grabbing the revolver before Abe could reach her. Spinning around as she snapped back the hammer, she lined the muzzle on her uncle's broad chest, and eyes wide with terror and rage, she warned, "Hold it right there or I'll shoot!" As she spoke, she retreated toward the back door.

Abe came on menacingly, rounding the table so that his bulky body blocked her path. He said nothing, and the bubbling, hissing sound of the boiling water on the stove filled the otherwise silent room.

Backing away from him and gripping the weapon in both hands, Lisa demanded, "Did you hear me? I said stop!"

Abe Washburn threw back his head and laughed as he slowly came closer. "You're gonna do what *I* say, or I'll kill you."

Lisa knew she had no choice. Gritting her teeth, she pulled the trigger—but the hammer made a hollow click on an empty chamber.

Laughing wickedly, Abe said, "Sorry to disappoint you, Lisa, but I emptied it as a little precaution. The gun didn't need to be loaded anyhow, since I was hardly worried that the killer would show up."

He suddenly lunged for her, and she screamed loudly, throwing the gun at him. Dodging his grasp, she turned to the stove and picked up the pot of boiling water and threw it at his face.

Abe howled and swore, staggering and raising his hands to his already blistering skin, and Lisa darted away from him out of the kitchen and toward the front door. She had almost reached the end of the hall when, with an angry roar, the massive man came at her again, and this time she could not escape him. Lisa screamed as his powerful hands seized her, holding her fast. Although she kicked at him with all her might, she could not break free.

Ben Bryce had raised his hand to knock when, hearing the screams, he stayed his hand, then threw his shoulder against the door, but it did not give at all. He tried it three more times, then realized it was bolted and the bolt was holding fast. Desperate, the lawman raced to the parlor window that looked out onto the end of the porch and kicked at the glass, shattering it. Disregarding the jagged shards clinging to the frame, he plunged through the opening into the room.

"Ben!" Lisa shouted, and Bryce looked toward the hallway and saw the young woman held captive in Abe Washburn's powerful arms.

As the lawman got to his feet, Abe threw Lisa aside so forcefully that she fell in a heap on the floor. Then the big man raced into the room, howling with rage that his carefully constructed plan had been destroyed. He lunged at the marshal, but Bryce dodged, and Abe rammed the wall. The huge man was thrown off balance, and the lawman sank his fingers into the blacksmith's shirt and slammed him into the wall, headfirst.

Abe dropped to his knees, swore, then stood up, shaking his enormous head. "I'm gonna kill you, Bryce!" he bellowed.

Before Ben Bryce had time to draw his revolver, Abe came at him. Drawing on every ounce of strength he had, the lawman threw a solid punch at the blacksmith, and the huge man's head whipped back from the blow. But he quickly regained his equilibrium and lashed out with a mighty punch of his own. Bryce sidestepped the blow slightly, but it still slammed into his shoulder with such force that the lawman feared it was dislocated.

Trading blows, the two men brawled for what seemed to Bryce an eternity, although he knew it was only moments. He caught a glimpse of Lisa sprawled on the floor in the hallway, her eyes wide with fear.

Abe was about to land another blow when the marshal threw himself on the floor, rolling into the huge man's feet, and Abe fell with a thud.

"Lisa!" Bryce shouted. "Unlock the front door!"

It was as if the sound of Ben Bryce's voice released the terrified young woman from a trance. Picking herself up, she staggered to the door, undoing the bolt. She then threw the door wide, and John Townsend and the other six men came rushing inside.

Abe Washburn loudly cursed Ben Bryce while getting to his feet, snarling, "I'm gonna snap your neck with my bare hands!"

But before he could carry out his threat, the seven men all jumped him, attempting to hold him down. When the blacksmith continued to fight, almost breaking free of his human bonds, Ben Bryce whipped out his revolver and clouted him savagely on the head. Abe's breath gushed out and he dropped, unconscious.

Lisa ran to Bryce as he slipped the gun back into its holster. Folding her into his arms as she broke into sobs of relief, he murmured, "It's all right now, my love. It's all right now."

At the trial a few days later the jury retired from the packed courtroom but needed only three minutes to deliberate before returning with their verdict. They found the accused, Abe Washburn, guilty of murder as charged, and the judge sentenced him to hang at sunrise the next day.

After locking the condemned killer in his cell, Marshal Ben Bryce walked Lisa home. Closing the door behind him, Bryce took her into his arms and kissed her. Then he held her at arm's length, looking into her eyes, and murmured, "Maybe it's not fair of me to ask you this right now, what with all the grief you're suffering, but I've got to return to El Paso now that this case has been solved, and, well, I don't want to leave without you." He paused, then grinned crookedly and remarked, "What I'm trying to say is, Lisa Washburn, will you marry me?"

Tears sprang into the young woman's blue eyes, and

she reached up and gently touched his cheek. "Oh, yes, my darling! Yes, I will!"

Kissing her, he declared, "Good! That means I'm officially the happiest man in the world."

Her eyes suddenly saddened and she shuddered slightly, admitting, "To tell you the truth, I can't wait to get away from Raton and leave all these terrible memories behind." Looking around her parlor, she added, "Of course, I'll be leaving a lot of happy ones, too—but it wouldn't be the same, living here and not having all my loved ones." Then she kissed Bryce and whispered, "But I *will* have my dearly beloved husband."

He kissed her tenderly, then murmured, "Truly the angels have smiled upon me."

Lisa giggled. "You mean because you are going to marry a rich woman, thanks to Great-Aunt Matilda?"

"Hmm," he retorted, a wry grin on his face, "I hadn't thought of that. But no, that's not what I'm referring to. Even without Aunt Matilda's money, I'm the luckiest man in the world because not only have I gotten a woman who loves me enough to marry me in spite of my badge, I also got the most beautiful woman to ever walk this earth."

"Flatterer!" she said, and laughed. Then, sighing contentedly, Lisa kissed him and announced, "I love you, Marshal Ben Bryce."

"And I love you, Lisa Washburn. And I hope it's not too many days before I can say, 'I love you, Lisa Bryce.' "

She snuggled into his arms. "Me, too. I like the sound of that."

The sun inched its way over the horizon, and Marshal Ben Bryce led a handcuffed Abe Washburn to the north end of Raton. Reaching the bottom of the knoll, the lawman saw that virtually the entire town had gathered to watch the hanging. Every eye was fixed on the big man as he slowly approached the gallows, and the townspeople, their faces filled with scorn, silently watched his progress, waiting for justice finally to be meted out.

With every successive step terror was more deeply etched on the blacksmith's face. The condemned man stiffened and stopped as he reached the staircase, as if physically unable to move. His eyes stared at the noose swaying slightly in the morning breeze, and he mumbled something incoherent.

Standing behind him, the lawman hissed, "I guess you need assistance up these steps."

Abe whipped his head around and faced Bryce. "Ben, please!" he begged. "Don't . . . don't make me do it! Any other way, but not the gallows!"

"Why not, Abe?" the marshal retorted. "Seems to me you should be thankful you've been sentenced to hang. After all, you did such a fine job of building this gallows, it works like a charm. A quick, clean death"—he paused and his face hardened—"not like the kind you inflicted on your victims." He prodded the big man in the back and snarled, "Move it!"

Abe Washburn's whole body began to tremble as he started slowly climbing the thirteen steps. His weakened knees gave way three times, and each time the marshal wrenched him to his feet and shoved him onward. The condemned man was bawling like a baby by the time he reached the platform, begging for forgiveness. When Bryce slipped the black hood from under his belt and shook it open, Abe started shaking violently, wailing, "No! No! No!"

His face as hard as stone, Bryce remarked icily, "I don't understand you, Abe. I'd have thought you'd be pleased to die this way. After all, you got what you wanted."

The big man stammered, "Wh-what are y-you talking about?"

Ignoring the question, Bryce dropped the hood over Abe Washburn's head, then lowered the noose and cinched it snugly around his neck. "Well," he finally answered, "when you were building this gallows, you told a lot of people you were eager to see your brother's killer die on it—so I guess you can take the drop as a happy man."